Close to the cab, Randi yelled behind her, "Don't even think about asking to drive my truck, Preacher Boy."

Matthew groaned inside. Yes, sir, trouble in more ways than one. He'd have to do some hard time on his knees trying to find a way to be grateful to God for throwing him into the hot seat. He'd almost been able to quit thinking about her every hour of the day, and now this. He looked up to see Randi staring at him. Her stance told him she was ready to battle for her right to drive.

"You have a look that says you could take on a whole football team without protective gear." Matthew smiled. "My sister looks like that when she's mad."

"My brother taught me everything I need to survive in a man's world."

"That explains why you drive a truck, I suppose," Matthew murmured.

"Excuse me?" Randi pulled her sunglasses from the V-neck of her T-shirt and slipped them on. "I didn't catch that."

"Nothing important." Matthew thought better of repeating himself.

DIANA LESIRE BRANDMEYER, a multipublished author, lives in Southern Illinois with her husband, Ed, and their cat, Wendell. They have three grown sons and a terrific daughter-in-law. Diana is a graduate of Webster University in St. Louis. She spends her spare time quilting, scrapbooking, bike riding, and reading, but not at the same time.

Hearts on
the Road

Diana Lesire Brandmeyer

Heartsong Presents

Dedication:
For my husband, Ed, champion of my dreams, and my mom, Audrey Ritter, who showed me the love of Christ and how to follow Him—no matter what.

Acknowledgments:
Thanks to Pastor Vern Lintvedt for truck stop lunches, Truckers for Christ, and Roger Miesner for help with the rig descriptions. Thanks also to my pre-readers, Sara Lesire and Barbara Friederich; your help is appreciated.

A note from the Author:
I love to hear from my readers! You may correspond with me by writing:

Diana Lesire Brandmeyer
Author Relations
PO Box 721
Uhrichsville, OH 44683

ISBN 978-1-60260-501-5

HEARTS ON THE ROAD

Our mission is to publish and distribute inspirational products offering exceptional value and biblical encouragement to the masses.

PRINTED IN THE U.S.A.

one

Sunshine caressed Randi Davis's face and poked its strong rays through her closed eyelids. Clawing her way back from the depths of sleep, she knew two things were wrong. The truck sat motionless, and it was past sunrise. "Jess, are you still sleeping?"

A grumble came from the bunk below. Jess Price, her partner, still huddled under blankets.

"Jess, wake up. We're late—again."

Covers rustled. The truck swayed gently with Jess's motion. "Late?" She groaned. "Now we're behind schedule. Why didn't you wake me up?"

"Don't yell at me. I did tell you to take over the wheel. You said okay. I assumed that meant you were. Good thing I didn't close the curtain; without the sun in my eyes, we might have slept for hours." Swinging her legs over the berth, Randi dropped to the floor and faced her driving partner of two years. "If you counted up the money we've lost from the times we've overslept, we could afford to take a cruise."

Jess dragged a brush through her hair. "You know Dana will be madder than a two-year-old told no."

"Yeah, I know." Randi yanked the canvas privacy curtain closed. Twisting around in the tight space to avoid Jess, she snatched a clean T-shirt from a small set of drawers in the corner of the sleeper cab. She slid it over her head. "Let's call the office after we eat. We can feel guilty with full stomachs instead of empty ones. She'll want us to leave now, forget breakfast. Besides, I need my caffeine jolt."

"Jolt?" Jess slipped on a leather boot. "More like submersion."

Randi agreed as she finished tying her tennis shoe. She

crawled over the driver's seat and opened the door. Grabbing the keys from the ignition and her cell phone, she jumped from the cab, wincing at the impact. The heat spiraled from the asphalt parking lot of the Wyoming Fuel and Go and curled its tentacles around her. After the coolness of the truck, she welcomed the warmth. The passenger door slammed with a bang. Randi turned, waiting for Jess.

"I'm starved." Jess ran her hand across her stomach as if to calm the beast within.

"And that's new?" Randi patted the emblem on the side of cab door. " 'Round the Clock' means we don't stop long. This has to be a fast breakfast, Jess. Not one of those famous 'I want one of everything' deals where you can't make up your mind."

"I know what I want." Jess propelled herself in the direction of the restaurant door, leaving soft taps from her cowboy boots hovering in the air.

Randi patted the back of her jeans, feeling for her wallet. "I forgot my money. Order me a large cappuccino and raspberry scones if they have them. If not, I'll take scrambled eggs."

"I love those dreams of yours. Better expect the eggs."

Randi turned back to the truck, slipping her fingers into her front pocket for the keys. Her reflection bounced back at her from the side of the polished door. Her hair resembled straw escaping from a bale. Looking for some kind of improvement, she gave it a quick finger comb.

Inside the truck, she reached under the driver's seat, her fingers grazing the smooth leather of her wallet. A stray lock of hair poked her in the eye. Grumbling at the aggravation, she wished she'd kept her salon appointment or at least brought along scissors. She removed one of many multicolored rubber bands resting on the neck of the stick shift and corralled her hair into a ponytail. Wallet in hand, she stepped onto the chrome running board and slammed the heavy truck door.

She scurried across the parking lot and pushed against the door of the truck stop. A blast of cold air from the ceiling vent sent shivers racing down her back. If they were on schedule, she'd go back for her warm shirt. She dreaded talking to Dana, the company dispatcher. Concentrating on a clever excuse, she came to an abrupt stop—against someone.

"Sorry! I didn't see you."

"That's okay." A voice warm enough to melt any iceberg wound its way through Randi.

"My fault. I wasn't paying attention." Randi stepped back to see what the brick wall she had smacked into looked like. She expected an overweight, unshaven trucker. Instead, delicious eye candy stood inches in front of her. Brown eyes met hers, and summer nights of stargazing suddenly seemed within her grasp. She knew deep inside she needed to get away from him. Fast. He made her feel too much, and he'd only said two words. Definite proof she had to give up watching classic Hepburn and Tracy movies.

"Are you hurt?" He reached out and caressed her arm.

She jerked her arm away. "Fine. I'm fine."

"Maybe I should stand back farther from the door. I'm Matthew Carter, by the way." He handed her a neon green sheet of paper.

"Thanks." Clutching the flyer, Randi fled, willing her face not to announce her inner turmoil, especially to Jess. She weaved around an aisle of mud flaps and yellow OVERSIZED LOAD signs into the attached restaurant. The top of Jess's red hair bobbed above a booth.

Randi slid into the booth, where a mug of coffee and Jess waited. She tossed the bright green page onto the center of the table with her phone then slid her hands around the mug, avoiding Jess's questioning look. She gulped the hot drink, wincing at the searing heat on her tongue. "Scones or eggs?"

"Eggs." Jess planted an elbow on the tabletop, propping her

chin on her palm. "What's going on?"

Randi grabbed the bundled silverware and uncurled the paper napkin. The utensils clunked against the Formica. She smoothed the napkin and placed it on her lap. "Nothing."

"Something's up. Why is your face red?" Jess nailed her with a stare. "What have you been doing?"

"I just bumped into that guy over there, that's all." Randi straightened her fork, knife, and spoon into exact parallel lines, avoiding direct contact with Jess's all-knowing eyes.

"Must have been some bump." Jess turned halfway in her seat and peered across the room. "Where is he?"

"He's over by the door in the gray T-shirt, holding a bunch of green paper. I walked right into him." Randi shook her head in disbelief.

Jess emitted a soft wolf whistle. "If you have to run into somebody, it's nice to run into a body like that." She sighed. "Makes me miss Mike all that much more."

Randi reached across the table and patted Jess's hand. "You'll be back with him in Cheyenne soon." Jess's face lit. Randi ached at her friend's happiness. She remembered that feeling; it's what she'd wished for her own life, but now that her thirtieth birthday had slid by, she'd made a different plan for herself. Independent Randi, that's who she wanted to be, not needing anyone or anything but the open road.

The waitress arrived with a tray. "Two breakfast specials with wheat toast, right?" She slid a plate of scrambled eggs in front of Randi.

"Thanks." Randi reached for the saltshaker as the waitress set down Jess's meal.

"Randi, I thought you agreed."

Her hand stilled. She had promised to pray with Jess or at least listen while Jess prayed before meals. It wasn't that she was opposed to God—more like He didn't seem interested in her. She folded her hands. "Say it fast, Jess. I'm hungry."

Jess arched an eyebrow in what Randi knew from experience was disapproval. "You know, you're going to make a great mom someday. You have the look down."

Jess said the common table prayer and finished with, "Father God, bring a good and God-loving man into Randi's life. Amen."

"Nice, Jess. You know that's not in my life plan anymore; it's going to be me and a truck till the end." Jess could have Mike. Randi hoped it would work out. *Maybe Mike is different from Brent.* Brent had promised Randi a life together, and that's what he'd meant. While she was home, they were together, but as soon as she left to student teach, he drove into another woman's driveway.

"I want you to have what I have with Mike; you deserve that." Jess flipped over the crumpled flyer with two fire-engine red fingernails. "So let's see what he's selling." Her eyes widened. "Randi, look at this picture. It's your guy. He's a minister."

"He's not mine." Randi snatched the paper and scanned the upcoming schedule of places where Matthew Carter would hold services. "He's preaching to truckers. Wonder if anyone shows up to hear him." She checked to see if he wore that better-than-thou pastor look. He didn't; he looked rather more like a man she might have considered dating once upon a time—before Brent reinforced an old lesson first taught by her father: Love can't be trusted.

Randi pushed her plate to the side then turned over the bill to check the total. "You want to call Dana?"

"No, but I will. She doesn't seem to appreciate your wit this early in the morning." Jess took a sip of her coffee. "And she's going to be in a bad mood when she finds out we're late."

Randi squished her napkin into a ball and placed it next to her plate. "I'll pay this and meet you back at the truck." She shot a glance at the front door. The man had left, or at least he wasn't standing there anymore. For a moment she felt disappointment, which confused her. Why did she care if he was still here?

As Randi breezed through the glass doors, her cell phone vibrated in her hand. "Hello?"

"Is this the correct number for Miranda Davis Bell?"

"Yes, this is Randi."

"My name is Rachel Miller. I'm with social services. Your brother's been arrested for making meth in his home. He listed you as a guardian for his daughter, Emma. When can we expect you to pick her up?"

two

Discouraged, Matthew gripped the bundle of flyers to his chest as he crossed the blistering parking lot. So far it hadn't been a good day for spreading the Word of God among the drivers. Most avoided him when he offered them a sheet.

"Wait up, Carter!"

Matthew turned to see one of the men who had recently begun attending his services. "Dirk. Didn't see you inside. Did you just get here?"

"Yeah, I ran into a mess. They shut down I-80 because some woman tried to make breakfast in their RV while it was moving. Caught the thing on fire."

"Did everyone get out?" Matthew shifted the stack of flyers in his arms.

"Yeah, the only fatality was breakfast." Dirk sputtered a laugh, smacking his knee with his hand. "Good one, huh? And no cursing, either."

"You did good, Dirk." Matthew slapped Dirk on the back in approval. Dirk's language had improved dramatically in the last month. He knew how hard it was for Dirk to give up his favorite adjectives, verbs, and nouns when he was surrounded daily by other drivers using those words freely.

"Yeah, but it's too bad about that couple losing their nice ride like that."

"You mean you weren't telling me one of your stories? This really happened?" He couldn't imagine the horror of watching your retirement home burn.

"I'm 'fraid so. It was one of those mega-expensive homes on wheels." Dirk nodded at the flyers Matthew held. "Any takers?"

"Not many." The image of the blond who'd smacked into him, smelling like summer, ballooned in his mind. She'd been the highlight of his morning.

"That's too bad. They don't know what they're missing." Dirk fell into step with Matthew as he walked to his pickup.

Matthew opened the door and backed away from the blast of heat that poured from the truck. "It's going to be a hot ride home." He tossed the flyers into a box overflowing on the floorboard.

"Once your air conditioner kicks in, you'll be all right." Dirk leaned against the side of the truck bed.

"It quit working about a month after the warranty expired." Matthew rolled down the window.

"Ooh doggie, that's rough. You need a new truck."

"I need another job. Hauling boats one way. . ." Matthew kicked at a lone pebble that had found its way onto the asphalt parking lot. It didn't roll far before it stopped against a wad of chewed gum someone had spat on the ground. "Anyway, I thought I'd be driving full-time by now."

"Who've you applied with? Just the big companies?" Dirk drummed his fingertips on the side of the truck bed.

"Everywhere, large and small. I even suggested I'd be a chaplain without pay."

"Free? How you going to eat and pay rent?" Dirk scratched his head above his ear, knocking his hat off center. "Nobody works for nothing."

"I meant for being a chaplain as an extra thing. They'd have to pay me for driving."

"Tell you what, give me your phone number. I'll talk to my dispatcher and see if there's any openings. Sometimes you need to know somebody to get in the door." Dirk tapped his chest with his thumb. "I'm *your* somebody."

"Thanks, Dirk. I'd appreciate that." Matthew wrote his number on a flyer and handed it to Dirk.

"All right, then. I gotta get back on the road." He straightened the bill of his black hat.

Matthew watched Dirk swagger toward his rig. A faint flutter of hope sprang inside him. Maybe this time God would answer his prayers.

❧

She should have realized A.J. was up to something. The last two times she'd asked to pick up Emma, her eight-year-old niece, for a 'girlie girl' day, he'd insisted on bringing Emma to her. Fury raged inside Randi.

How could A.J. be so stupid? Drugs. Again. And this time producing them in his home, while his daughter slept in the other room. This time they wouldn't hesitate to honor him with a well-deserved extended stay in prison.

Climbing into the truck, she slammed the door. She tried to swallow her anger, but it stuck in her throat, embedded in the thickened embarrassment her brother had caused.

Jess sat behind the wheel. She adjusted the side mirror on the driver's side. "You call the next time we oversleep."

Randi chose her words with care, trying to keep her emotions about A.J. from entering the discussion. "What did Dana say?"

"The usual. Any more delays and she's going to short us on trips."

Randi snapped her seat belt. "She can't do that."

Jess pushed a button and held it for twenty seconds to warm the glow plugs. She turned the key, and the diesel started with a roar. "She knows that. She had to say something so she'll feel like she's in charge. I told her not to get her panties in a knot; the truck will be back in the yard before night."

"True—we both slept through the night, so we can drive straight through." Randi leaned her head back on the headrest. "It's going to be a long day."

"She also said to be careful because a trucker has been shot."

Randi shivered. "Where?" A crazy with a gun who didn't like truckers might be enough to make anyone think about switching careers.

"Colorado, a drive-by at the rest stop. They haven't caught the shooter yet." Jess maneuvered the truck through the parking lot. "Seems the guy stayed on the highway and shot through the passenger window of his car."

"Sounds like he's mad at somebody. Dana didn't say if it was an east or west stop, did she?" Randi worked the rubber band out of her hair. She reached into the door cubby and pulled out a brush.

"I didn't think to ask." Jess steered the slowly rolling truck onto the highway entrance ramp. "Saw you on the phone. Who called?"

"A. J.'s in jail." Randi stared out the window. "He wants me to take Emma."

Jess whipped her head around. "Are you going to?"

"She can live with my mom." In her stomach, the scrambled eggs from breakfast slammed into the toast.

"Do you think that's fair to your mom? She's not been well, Randi."

Randi bristled at Jess's words. "I suppose not, but for now it's better than being put into the foster care system."

"Randi! You're her aunt. You wouldn't do that to Emma, would you?"

Randi stared at the road ahead. "I don't know what else I could do. I'm never home. How can I take care of her?"

"You could teach, Randi. You did get your degree."

"But it's not what I want to do. Teaching was part of the plan with Brent. That didn't work."

"Maybe God is giving you another plan to follow."

❧

Standing in the doorway of her mother's kitchen, Randi held her ground. "I can't. She can't live with me, Mom. I drive a

truck for a living. I can't change my life for my brother's kid."
As soon as the words tripped off her tongue, she regretted
them, grateful Emma was at her friend's home for the night.
They would pierce her like a knife.

Her mother plunged her hands into the soapy water,
scrubbed a pot for a moment, then banged it on the drain
board to dry. She turned and wiped her hands with a yellow-
and-blue-striped dish towel. Her lips stretched in a tight line.

Randi's shoulders tightened. She knew the look on her
mom's face. She'd seen it many times. A long spell of talking
about what's wrong and what's right was about to start. She
didn't want to hear it. She needed to go home, get some sleep,
and then think about what to do—tomorrow.

"You're her godmother, Randi."

"Exactly. I'm supposed to be praying for her—which I
do—and make sure she goes to church—which I haven't
since I don't have a church anymore."

"You could have one."

"Don't get going, Mom. I know what you're going to say,
but what's so wrong about Emma living with you? You have
an extra bedroom, and Emma will be around to keep you
company, watch movies with you. . . Remember how we
watched movies together? You'd make popcorn and sprinkle
it with cheese, and we'd sit on the couch with Grandma's
quilt spread over our laps." For a moment she longed for that
feeling of belonging, knowing someone wanted to hear about
her day.

"I won't forget those times, not ever, Miranda Davis Bell.
But my time for raising kids has done passed. I'm old and
I'm tired. I don't want to stay up late helping an eight-year-
old build villages out of cardboard or practice spelling words.
I don't need the worry, either. Being a parent today can't be
easy, and being Emma's parent will be even harder." Mrs. Bell
scooted a wooden chair from the kitchen table. "Sit down

and talk to me. Maybe you'll change your mind."

"I won't, Mom. I have student loans I'm still paying, and you know driving doesn't pay very much. Quitting my job and moving into a two-bedroom isn't possible. I'll come and get her when I'm home. It's a win-win situation." Randi couldn't help but notice how thin her mom was. She must not be cooking meals for herself. If Emma were here, her mother would have to cook again. This could be good for her mom. Randi's mood brightened. Maybe her mom needed a little more time to think about keeping Emma. "I'd like to stay and chat, Mom, but I need to get home. I need to get bills paid tonight so I can mail them tomorrow."

"This isn't going to go away. Emma needs a home, either with you or the state. Maybe you could use that teaching degree instead of driving." Her mother sighed. "Guess there's no discussing it with you tonight."

"Mom, I made my choice. I like what I'm doing." Randi turned to leave. Her mom needed a night to think about having her granddaughter with her all the time. How many times had she heard her mom wishing her children were still small? Emma could fill that need.

"Just one more thing."

Randi stopped at the doorway. Her mom didn't plan to let her leave without something to think about. She never did. "What? You want me to pray about this, don't you?"

"Yes."

"That's it, then? Just pray about my decision?" It amazed Randi how her mother depended on God to direct everything in her life. Couldn't her mother make a decision on her own, just once? Still, for a moment, she longed to feel she could do the same.

three

Randi drove her car into the only open spot, next to the huge green garbage bin. Its lid gaped, gripping a white plastic bag between its metal lips. *Home.* It didn't feel like one, but at least she wouldn't have to wait at a truck stop for her number to be called for a shower. From the backseat she collected her duffel bag, slinging it over her shoulder before slamming the door.

Overhead lights threw shadows from the trees bordering the street across the rough concrete sidewalk. The third step down to her basement apartment had lost more of its sharp concrete edge. The night-sensitive porch light flickered over her doorway like a sign from an old roadside diner. Timing its flashes, she managed to insert her key into the lock. Grasping the knob, she hesitated. Nothing really waited for her inside. *Maybe I should—should what? Bring Emma to live with me? I love Emma, but I'm not her best option.*

Inside she dropped her bag onto the floor and slid three dead bolts across the closed door. That enforced her decision. She couldn't bring Emma to live in this place. She reached over and twisted the switch at the base of the lamp next to the door. The harsh glare from the high-wattage bulb assaulted the room. The burgundy slipcover on the couch sagged, exposing a worn shoulder where a previous owner's cat had exercised its claws. With a swift tug, Randi positioned it in place.

She retrieved the few pieces of mail on her floor. Nothing but offers for credit cards. The musty smell she associated with homecoming after weeks on the road needed banishing. The first thing she would do was to light the scented candle Jess gave her last Christmas—was it seashore or forest? Something like that. Taking two steps, she stopped at the coffee table and dropped the mail next to the candle. Matchbooks collected from truck stops across the country formed a heap in a small ceramic bowl. She picked one and withdrew a match, struck it, and touched the flame to one of the three candle wicks. She blew out the match and laid it on a small heart-shaped dish. And noise. This place needed some. Scooping up the remote, she switched on the television. The news channel filled the screen, and the quiet dissipated.

Randi slipped off her sandals and tossed them into a basket by the door. She headed for the shower, pausing when the newscaster's words "rest stop" and "shot" caught her attention. Wheeling around, she tried to pick up the story, hoping they were offering more information than she and Jess had heard when they'd returned the truck. After a few seconds it was apparent they had nothing new to offer.

❧

After her shower, she grabbed a soda from her fridge and a bag of chips from the cabinet. Settling onto the couch, she spread a blanket over her lap. The remote in her hand, she flipped through the channels. Maybe she could find a good movie tonight. Black and white flashed across the screen. She stopped. Good, a classic. They were the best, always taking her to another time, when the biggest stress in her life was a math test.

A curly-haired child in an orphanage danced across the screen proclaiming she would be okay. Her daddy would come for her; she just knew he would.

That could be Emma. She blinked back tears and hardened her heart against the bludgeoning of loneliness and guilt. *Great. Mom must be praying.* She continued scrolling through the extensive channel list for something else, even an infomercial. Her finger paused as a man sopping with sweat screamed at his audience, "Just come to God with your problems. He can solve everything."

The camera zoomed in on the man's glistening face. "Listen to your heart. Just give your troubles to Him," he whispered. "You know God can hear you. He wants you and your love. He's waiting for you. What are you waiting for?"

Randi felt his piercing glare through the screen. She squirmed, wondering if her mom had somehow managed to broadcast this man into her home, like some kind of science fiction. Mesmerized, she listened a bit longer.

She tossed the blanket to the floor. Maybe she should talk to a pastor. But who? She hadn't attended church since she started driving; it wasn't as if truckers were welcomed—or at least not their trucks. There always seemed to be a sign saying No Semi Parking Allowed.

"Call us now. What are you waiting for?" the voice from the television urged.

What did she have to lose? Leaning over the arm of the couch, she snatched the phone from the floor and punched in the 888 number. A computer voice asked if she was dialing from a touch-tone phone. If so, please press 1; if not, please stay on the line.

"Oh no, you don't. I'm not playing the number punch bingo tonight. Besides, this shouldn't happen to a person in need of prayer." Randi waited for a real person to answer.

"Please wait. One of our student disciples will be with you soon."

"Sure they will." Randi soon hummed along with the canned gospel music. She glanced at the clock on the windowsill. Five minutes passed. *Must be a lot of people in need of guidance tonight,* she thought. Nestling the phone on her shoulder, she counted to ten once then started over. She made it to seven.

"This is Angelica. May I have your name?"

She paused for a moment, unsure about giving any personal

information. First name should be safe. "Randi."

"Hi, Randi. What can I help you with this evening?" Angelica's silken voice massaged Randi's tensed nerves.

"I've been asked to do something that would upturn my entire life. My niece needs—"

"Can you hold? I'd like to transfer you to someone more skilled than I to pray with you."

Someone more skilled in prayer? Did they have levels of prayer people? What did this woman get to pray for? Lost keys? And how did they test for praying skills? "Sure, I suppose."

"Can I have your phone number and address?"

"Why do you need those?"

"In case we get disconnected, we can call you back."

"That explains the phone number, but not the address. You aren't planning on coming over tonight to personally pray with me, are you?"

"We'd like to send you information about our ministry. We don't do house calls." Angelica's voice went from silky to thorny.

"You mean to ask me for a donation?" So much for free help; maybe this church thought money made the prayers reach God faster.

"There will be an envelope included for that purpose if you wish."

"I don't think so." Randi ended the call feeling more alone than before.

❧

The sunset cast a rosy glow over the parking lot of Boats and Moor as Matthew unplugged the trailer lights. Standing on top of the dualie tire, he stretched over the side of his truck to reach the gooseneck hitch in the middle of the truck bed and released the latch. At the snap of metal, he dropped down to the pavement. Noticing a now-clean swipe on the side of the truck, he glanced down and grimaced at the dirt smeared across his favorite 'Pokes T-shirt. He brushed it off, but a shadow of dirt remained, much like the shadow of the Wyoming Cowpokes' last game. His last clean shirt, and he was two days from home.

"Carter."

"Kennedy. I'll get your paperwork. You'll save me a trip inside." Matthew reached into the truck and grabbed a clipboard off the bench seat.

Tom Kennedy ran his hand along the prow of the speedboat. "Looks like you brought me a nice one today."

Matthew walked over next to him. "Here you go." He handed the clipboard and pen to Tom. "Sign by the Xs. She is a beautiful boat. I'm sure the new owner will love her."

Tom signed the papers and handed them back to Matthew. "I'm just about to close for the day. The wife's at her mom's, so I'm free for dinner if you want company at your table tonight."

"Yeah, I'd like that, but I'm pretty dirty," Matthew said.

"I know a great place where as long as you're decent they feed you. And I don't care if you've been rolling in mud." Tom inspected his own hands. "I'm not all that clean, either. The grease under my nails isn't going to disappear before dinner."

Inside the store, Matthew waited for Tom to close out his cash register and put his money in the safe. "Pretty trusting to do that while I'm in here, aren't you?"

"I have nothing to worry about with you. It's like having God stand behind me."

"Don't hold me up next to God. I'm no better than any other sinner."

Tom locked the door. "I know, but some people are safer than others. You can't deny that fact."

"I won't." Matthew's stomach rumbled. "Where are we eating?"

"Dandee Inn. It's just up the road on the left. Want to ride along with me?"

"Sure, if you don't mind bringing me back for my truck later. I could use the rest time. I'm planning on starting back after we eat."

Tom jumped into his pickup. He turned the key and the radio screamed to life.

Matthew startled then recognized the sounds of a popular Christian praise band. "Great sound."

"Sorry about that. I like my music loud." Tom lowered the volume.

"Me, too—drowns out the road noise that makes me drowsy."

"Don't you get tired of living out of your truck?"

"Sometimes."

"So why do you keep doing it? I'll hire you; then you can settle in, find a good wife, and have a couple of kids."

"I'm not ready to settle. Not yet. God has called me for His purpose—to teach others about Him. I'm just waiting on Him to get me into the right company where I can do that."

"But if that's what He wants, then why aren't you traveling across the country with a rolling church, like Truckers for Christ?"

"I don't know. I ask that question all the time."

"Maybe you're confused on your purpose. Maybe instead of asking, you should be listening."

"Well said, but I'm not ready to give up my dream yet."

Tom raised an eyebrow. "Your dream? I thought it was God's plan."

"It is. I'm sure it is. It will happen when the timing is right." Matthew tried to silence the questions rising in his mind. What if he had misread God's intention? What if he was following his own path instead of God's?

four

Randi rounded the back of the truck to finish the pre-ride check. The trailer door didn't budge when she pulled on it. The signal lights were both flashing. They were ready to roll. She kicked the back tire of her cab with the toe of her boot. *Ritual completed, check.* With one foot resting on the running board, she climbed into the truck where Jess waited. "Ready?"

"I suppose. I didn't sleep well last night. I must be coming down with something." Jess yawned. "Leaving Mike for two weeks isn't fun."

"At least this way you don't have time to get bored with each other." Randi started the engine. The click of the diesel engine welcomed her back. The sound never failed to bring her joy. She was born for this. A quick look at the gauges assured her everything measured where it should.

"I hope he doesn't." Jess crossed her arms over her chest and frowned. "As long as he doesn't get tired of waiting for me to get back."

"Come on, Jess. You know he isn't going to mess around with anyone. Not Michael. He's one of the good ones. Besides, when would he have time? He has too much studying to do. Doesn't he?"

"Lots of book work this week, anyway. Taking that bar exam next month has him worried. He thinks he won't pass." Jess picked a piece of lint off her capri pants and flicked it in the trash bag attached to a hook on the dash.

"Why? He's smart enough." Leaving the truck terminal, Randi shifted into a higher gear.

"He keeps being told by other lawyers that no one passes it

23

the first time. Mike thinks he has to be better than the rest. I don't doubt he'll pass it the first time." Jess retrieved her log book and pen from the cubby on the door and wrote down the date. "I know I don't want to be around if he doesn't. Remind me to make sure we can take a load the week the results are supposed to come back." She slid the book back into the space on the door.

"Some supporting wife you're going to make." Randi laughed. "Where's your 'stand by your man' philosophy?"

"Please. Stand by your man? You've been listening to that old country station again. I fully intend to be a good wife, but I'm not married to him yet."

"I think you will be."

"Probably. Maybe. I don't know, Randi. Maybe he's not the one. Maybe I should reconsider one of those guys we met last spring at Anne's Date-a-Minute party."

Randi frowned. She had politely smiled and asked questions for hours that night. At the end of the evening, her tally sheet remained blank. None of those men held any interest for her. She'd gone only because Jess and Anne begged. Randi told them she wasn't interested. She didn't plan to settle down with a husband, ever. "Do you really think any of them are as promising as Mike? He's going to have a great career, and he's crazy about you."

"Maybe. He's said he loves me, but I want to make sure." Jess twisted around in the seat to face Randi. "You didn't call. Tell me what happened with Emma. Is she living with you now?"

"No, not now. She's at Mom's, but Mom said she can't stay. I don't know what's going to happen with her." Randi accelerated to pass a pickup dangerously overloaded with furniture topped with a mattress.

"What do you mean, you don't know?"

"It's not that I don't want to take Emma." Randi paused,

searching for the right words. "If I take her, my entire life will have to change."

"And hers hasn't been changed?"

"Of course it has. But I don't even have a bedroom for her, and my lease isn't up for another five months."

"What other choice is there?"

"If Mom won't keep her?" Randi steeled herself for Jess's reaction. She knew how Jess felt about family, but Randi knew from firsthand experience that you can't depend on people who have the same last name. Better Emma learn now than later. "She goes into the foster care system until I can get another place to live and a different job. It's overwhelming."

Jess reached for her stainless steel coffee mug from the cup holder on the floor. "But isn't she worth changing your life for?" The steel mug settled with a clunk in the cup holder as Jess suddenly doubled over with a whimper.

Randi took her foot off the accelerator. Jess's face glistened with sweat.

"What's wrong?"

"I don't know," Jess said. "No. I feel awful. There's a rest stop coming up. Can we stop for a minute? Maybe if I splash my face with cold water. . . I'm just going to put my head down until we get there. I feel light-headed."

Randi's heart raced. Should she call for help? She wasn't quite sure Jess knew what was best for Jess. Stopping would be the best choice. From there Randi could call for help if she needed to.

"I'll be okay." Jess's muffled voice floated up to Randi. "Might be food poisoning. We ate at a new place last night, and I had chicken."

The cab filled with silence as Randi drove. The familiar blue sign with its white picnic table flashed by the window. "The rest stop is coming up, Jess. Just another minute or two." Randi's mouth felt dry. *Food poisoning? What do you do for that?*

The exit appeared none too soon for Randi. A quick glance at the lot and she knew she'd have to park on the edge of the lot. She gripped the Jake Brake and pulled; the rat-a-tat sound of the engine compression braking system rattled her nerves. "We're here, Jess. Do you think you can walk?"

Jess sat up but anchored her head in her hands as if it might float away. "I'm better, I think, now that the truck is stopped." She popped open the door. "Maybe walk next to me?"

"Wait for me, then." Randi sprinted around the cab to help.

Jess put a foot on the running board. "I think—"

Pop. Whish. Glass shattered around her.

Jess screamed and fell on Randi, knocking her to the ground.

Jess went limp and silent.

"Jess! Are you okay?" Randi rolled Jess off her then scooted along the ground close to her.

"I hurt. My arm. It hurts." Jess began to moan.

A dark, wet stain began to form around a gaping hole in Jess's black T-shirt. Bile rose in Randi's throat; she swallowed. The sight of Jess's face, white as skim milk, impaled her with fear.

"I think you've been shot."

five

The flashing lights of another police car pierced the gray day. Randi shook and her teeth banged together. She tried to stop both the shivering and the chattering. She tried hard. She'd tried all her life not to be weak, but this she couldn't stop.

Everything happened so fast. She didn't remember how she got to the curb where she sat. Someone draped a rough gray blanket around her shoulders. It covered her to her feet, but it didn't ease the chill that had settled deep inside. Jess had blood on her shirt; that she knew. Who called the police? And when did the ambulances arrive? She clutched the blanket tighter.

"Are you getting any warmer?"

She became aware of the man sitting close beside her. She thought she knew him, but from where? The memory kept floating out of reach. "No." He seemed familiar, but she couldn't think of his name. "Who are you?"

"Matthew. Matthew Carter. You're still cold. I'll go see if I can find another blanket." He started to stand.

She grabbed his arm. "Don't go. Tell me what happened."

"Can I put my arm around you? That might help to warm you."

She hesitated. Another fierce shiver ran through her. "Okay." Her voice quivered. "Please tell me about Jess."

"She was with you, right?" Matthew pulled her a little closer and rubbed her arm, as though trying to dispel her chills. "I don't know what happened. I pulled in a few minutes ago. I only know she's been shot and you're bleeding."

"I'm bleeding? Did I get shot, too?" Her fingers fumbled

across her chest. Did she have a hole in her? Visions of blood pumping from her assailed her mind.

Matthew drew her closer, anchoring her shaky arm with his firm one. "No. I don't think you've been shot. Randi, it's going to be okay."

Someone squatted in front of her. "Randi? My name is Bill. I'm a paramedic and I'm going to help you. I need to look at your face right now."

"Is Jess dead?" Her words seemed to float over her head, and she wondered if she had even said them aloud.

"She's alive. They'll be taking her to the hospital soon. You'll follow in the other ambulance." He gently brushed her hair from her face and patted it with something cool.

"Why can't I go with Jess? I haven't been shot, have I?" She started to rise, feeling the need to get her control back. Pain shot between her eyes, and she hunched over, pulling away from Matthew. "I–I'm fine. I just need to get to Jess."

"You're lucky you weren't shot like your partner, Randi. But pieces of glass hit you in the face. We have to make sure all the pieces are removed, and I can't do that here."

"Then I'll go with Jess. I have to ride with her. I'm her partner." She tried to stand, but her eyes wouldn't focus. She felt light-headed, as if she had sucked a balloon full of helium. Her legs began to wobble.

Matthew reached out and steadied her. He helped her sit back down on the curb. "Maybe in a minute you'll be stronger."

"You can't ride with her, Randi. They need the room to help her." Bill cleaned her face with something that smelled like the stuff her mom used to put on her scraped knees when she'd fallen rollerblading.

The blanket slipped from her shoulder. Matthew draped it back into place. "Is there someone you want me to call? Someone you want to have at the hospital when you get there?"

"Mom is too far away to come, and I don't want to scare her. Tell me about Jess. How bad is she? Tell me the truth."

"I don't know, Randi."

"I can't feel anything. Are you sure I'm hurt?" Randi searched Bill's face for any clues about how badly she'd been cut.

"Lots of little cuts. You're lucky you didn't get any glass in your eyes."

"Miss Bell?"

Randi pivoted her head. A Wyoming state patrol officer stood in front of her. "That's me."

"I'm Officer Benfield." The leather holster around his waist crackled as he bent down in front of her. "I need to ask you what you saw."

"Nothing. Nothing at all." The need to give him details weighed heavy like granite on her shoulders. "I didn't see a car or truck or van. Nothing. Not even the sound of an engine."

Officer Benfield stood. "Maybe in a little while a detail will come to you."

"I can't tell you anything." Randi's teeth chattered.

"Let's get her inside the ambulance," Bill said. "You can send someone to talk to her at the hospital."

"I didn't even know Jess had been shot until I saw the. . ." She attempted to stand but sank back to the curb. "Blood."

"Miss Bell, someone will be in contact with you later today. I'm sorry this incident occurred."

Incident? That's what he thought this was? This was life changing, and if she weren't so tired, she would tell him so.

Matthew helped her to her feet. "I'd like to come with you."

"With me?" She stared at the pavement, her thoughts folding over each other in slow motion. Why would he want to? She shivered and felt his arm on hers. But the bigger question. . . *Why do I want him to?*

"Sorry, sir, no extra riders are allowed." Bill snapped his

medical case shut. "You could follow her, though."

"Randi?" Matthew squeezed her hand. "You shouldn't be alone."

"You can come," she whispered.

૨ઠ

At the hospital, Bill and another paramedic wheeled Randi into a curtained room next to an exam table where a nurse waited. "I'm Sue, and I'll be taking care of you."

Randi propped herself up on her elbow. "Can you tell me what's happening with my partner?"

Sue grasped Randi's wrist between her fingers and took her pulse. "What's her name? I'll try to find out for you."

"Jess Price. Someone shot her."

"You first. Can you remove your shirt, or would you like me to help you?"

"I can do it." Randi looked down to unbutton the blood-soaked shirt. Jess's or hers? Her head swam in misty darkness. Taking a deep breath, she peeled the fabric away from her skin.

Sue opened a cabinet and retrieved a gown covered in a tiny geometric pattern. She held it out to Randi. "Put this on." She took Randi's shirt from her. "Do you want to keep this? I can put it in a plastic bag for you."

"No." Randi shook her head in distaste. She would never wear that shirt again.

"I wouldn't want to keep it, either. I'll try to find you something to wear home." She tossed the shirt in the trash receptacle.

"Can you see if Matthew Carter is here yet?"

"Sure." Sue spun on her heels and left the room.

A moment later, she returned with the doctor and Matthew. Randi answered a few questions while Sue took notes, and then the doctor aimed a bright light on her face. He placed a magnifying visor over his eyes. "I'll try to be gentle, but I'm afraid a few of these might sting. I have something to numb your face."

"No, thanks. I can do this. Will I need stitches?"

"Possibly. I'll know soon. You tell me if this is too painful. If it is, I'll stop and get you numb." She glanced down at his ID tag as Dr. Simon proceeded to remove a small sliver of glass.

Randi jerked. "Ow." Tears stung her eyes.

Matthew squeezed her hand. "I think you should give her something."

"Should I stop?" Dr. Simon's hand paused in the air.

"How many more?"

"Enough, and I have to get in deep for some of these. I think I should give you something to ease the pain."

"But I won't be able to drive."

"I don't think you'll be driving anywhere tonight, anyway. Why not get relief for the pain?"

Randi panicked. "I don't have anything to drive, do I? Where's my truck?"

"It's taken care of." Matthew's voice softened. "I think you should let them deaden the pain."

"It does hurt more than I thought." She sniffed, hating to give in.

Dr. Simon nodded to Sue. He took the prepared needle she offered. After the injections, Randi's face stiffened with numbness.

The doctor finished removing the last piece of glass and dropped it with the rest in a stainless steel dish. "That's the last of it. Only one more thing for me to do. A few stitches on your forehead. Don't worry. It isn't going to leave a scar. I think you might have rubbed it, causing it to tear."

"I don't remember doing that."

"Well, that's not unusual." Dr. Simon knotted the thread.

Randi closed her eyes, not wanting to see the approaching needle.

"All done," he said a moment later. "Sue will give you a paper with directions for taking care of your cuts, along with a prescription for pain pills. If you have any problems, go see your regular doctor."

"Can I go back to work?"

"Take a couple of days off. You've been through a stressful event, and your body needs to recover." Dr. Simon ripped off his latex gloves with a snap and tossed them into the trash can. "Take care," he said as he left the room.

Sue patted her on the back and offered a smile. "I found a T-shirt from one of the drug companies." She handed her the folded white shirt.

"Thanks. I can send it back."

"No need." The nurse handed her a stack of papers. "Read these and sign at the bottom. Then you can go." She glanced at Matthew. "Would you step outside so she can change? Then you can be a good boyfriend and take care of her tonight."

"I will." Matthew winked at Randi.

Sue closed the curtain and waited for Randi to put on the T-shirt. "And, Randi, an officer wants to ask you a few more questions before you leave. After you talk to him, you'll find your friend on the fourth floor. She's in surgery now. You can wait in the surgical waiting room up there." As Randi signed her release papers, Sue slid open the curtain and allowed the officer inside. "She's ready to talk to you now."

"I'm Officer Perkins; this shouldn't take long."

"I don't have any new information to add." Randi handed the clipboard back to Sue.

Officer Perkins flipped open a notebook cover. "Just in case you've forgotten something, why don't you tell me what you saw."

"Nothing. I didn't see anything. I walked around the front of the truck, and when I opened the door for Jess, I heard a noise, and then Jess had blood all over her shirt."

"You didn't see a car or truck pulling away or hear tires squealing?"

"No, nothing. I wish I had seen something."

Officer Perkins retrieved a card from his pocket then closed his notebook. "If you do think of anything, no matter how small, you can call us, all right?" He slipped the card into her hand.

Randi faltered at the doorway when she saw Matthew waiting for her. She brushed past him and headed for the elevator.

"Hey, Randi, wait."

She pushed the UP button then turned and faced him, her hands scrunched in tight fists by her sides. "Boyfriend? I don't even know you."

"Technically, we've met before."

"When? I don't remember."

"You ran into me at the Fuel and Go. I handed you a flyer and told you my name. You didn't tell me yours until I asked you at the rest area. I remembered your eyes. They're—"

"I know. Family trait." That had created a host of problems on the playground. "You're the preacher? You look different."

"I haven't shaved." He rubbed his chin. "I'm on my way back from dropping off a boat."

"So you're here because it's the 'pastorly' thing to do?" The elevator doors behind her remained closed. She wondered if taking the stairs might be faster.

"At first, but now that I've been introduced to your charming wit, I'd like to stick around awhile. At least long enough to make sure you get home safely."

"I don't date pastors." The prayer hotline had wanted more from her than she wanted to give. Did Matthew as well? She moved a little farther away from him, not all that comfortable with those mocha eyes staring down at her. Why? Because he was a pastor? Or because she found him attractive?

He smiled at her. "Actually, I'd like to make sure you're okay. Besides, you do need a ride home, right?"

She swallowed hard and nodded, willing the telltale warmth in her cheeks to fade and the ding of the elevator to sound.

"Good. Then it's settled. I'll fill the role of a big brother until you can take over. Then after we check on Jess, why not let me drive you home?"

"I don't know. I guess I can trust you, but isn't that going out of your way? You'll lose paid driving time."

"I'm on my way back, and I don't have another delivery set up. Where do you live?"

"Torrington."

"I'm just on the east side of there. I can take you home, or at least help you get settled in a hotel nearby."

She looked up, the blush finally breaking through to heat her cheeks to roasting temperature. "If Jess doesn't need me." She punched the Up button several more times, willing the elevator to open up and deliver her.

Matthew leaned against the wall with a satisfied smile in place. "Good. We'll check on Jess and then head for home."

Randi caught his gaze, noting the twinkle in his eyes. "Thanks. I guess you take that Good Samaritan thing seriously."

"You bet. 'Love thy neighbor' is my motto."

A sharp ding jolted her back to reality as the elevator doors eased open. Randi ducked inside, feeling grateful the walls weren't mirrored. She hadn't prayed for herself in a long time, but something whispered that Matthew was her answer to a long-ago, almost forgotten prayer.

❧

The elevator doors slid open again, exposing polished floors. Fluorescent lighting bounced against the hard shine of the dark green tile. A blue arrow directed visitors around the corner to the surgical waiting room.

Randi stopped at the doorway. If she went inside, this would be real. She didn't have time to think it though, as Matthew, his hand at her elbow, propelled her into the room.

A pink-smocked volunteer sat behind a desk. Below her laminated name tag hung a picture of an infant with the corny phrase ASK ME ABOUT MY GRANDDAUGHTER emblazoned below it. "Who are you waiting for?"

"Jess." Behind her, someone on television yelled out a letter then screamed. Randi cringed, wondering how normal life could continue when so much had happened. Shouldn't the world have changed? "Jess Price. Do you know what's happening with her?"

"Are you a relative?" The volunteer didn't look up from the counted cross-stitch she held on her lap.

"No, but we work together. We're like sisters."

She glanced up at them. "I can't tell you what her condition is. The privacy act doesn't allow me to give out information to a nonrelative." She looked down, pulled her thread through, and prepared to take another stitch. "How do you know she's even here? They aren't supposed to give out that information downstairs."

Randi leaned on the edge of the desk, placing her hands over the counted cross-stitch chart spread on top. "We were together when someone shot her. You have to tell me."

The volunteer scooted her chair back. "No, I don't."

"Randi, you're scaring the woman." Matthew gently turned her around and led her to a row of plastic chairs. "Why don't you sit here and rest?"

Randi plopped into one. She would sit because she wanted to, not because he'd told her to.

Matthew stared at her for a moment, looking confused. Too bad. He hadn't done anything wrong, but she didn't want him to think she needed him. She watched him go back to the volunteer. Now what? Did he think he could charm information out of that woman?

"So how old is your granddaughter?"

"She's four days old." The woman grinned at him.

"She's cute. Have you been able to hold her yet?"

"No, but next week I'm flying out to Georgia. I'll be helping her parents, and I'm planning on holding that little one often."

Randi couldn't believe the change in that woman. Matthew had some kind of magic, getting her to beam like that.

"Who did you say you're here for?" the volunteer asked Matthew.

"Jess Price."

"I'm not supposed to say anything, but since you know she's here, just this once." The woman looked over her shoulder as if to make sure no one would catch her bending the rules. "She's still in surgery. They said it would be about three hours before her family could see her."

"Thank you, ma'am. My. . .my friend might be able to rest now."

Randi saw Matthew turn. She quickly closed her eyes, not willing to let him know she'd watched his every slick move. He sat next to her and touched her hand.

"Can I get you something?"

"No, thank you." Her voice was as stiff as cardboard.

"Did you hear what she said about Jess?"

"Yes." And the part about being her friend, and the way he said it, implicating she was more than a friend. Didn't it? She still reeled from the boyfriend comment in the ER. He should have said something. He was a pastor, wasn't he? She closed her eyes. Maybe if she ignored him, he would go away. She'd find another way home.

The adrenaline swell from earlier had dissipated, leaving exhaustion in its wake. She leaned her head against the wall and soon fell asleep. When she woke, she looked around.

Something was missing. No, someone. Matthew was gone, and she felt a sense of abandonment. Then she noticed Mike, Jess's boyfriend. He paced the waiting room floor. "Hey."

Mike turned. "I didn't want to wake you when I arrived. I thought you might need to rest. Are you okay? I met Matthew. He said you were cut and needed stitches."

"Just a few in my forehead. I'm lucky none of the glass hit my eyes." She blinked away the cloud of drowsiness surrounding her mind.

She shot out of her chair. "Jess! Tell me about Jess. They wouldn't tell me anything because I'm not related." She scowled. "I'm her partner. We drive a truck together. We see each other more than most sisters do." She wanted to rub her face. Where the numbness was wearing off, she felt prickles below the surface.

"I know. When the hospital called her parents, they told them to consider me family since we're engaged and they couldn't get here as fast as I could."

Randi blinked hard. "Engaged?"

Mike grinned. "Last weekend. We're getting the ring the next time she has a weekend off. She didn't tell you?"

"No." And she wasn't about to tell him what Jess did say.

"I think she wanted to wait until we made it official with a ring."

Randi hoped that was the reason, but right now she wanted Jess to be okay. "How is she?"

"Still in recovery, but the doctor came in earlier and said she'll be fine. They took a bullet out of her shoulder. None of the bone shattered." He checked his watch, giving it a tap as if to make the time go faster.

"She was sick before—before she was shot. Did they find out what was wrong with her?"

"They think it was caused by our celebration dinner."

"Jess did mention the chicken. I'm glad it wasn't something

else. She'll have enough to deal with now. Can she leave soon?"

"Maybe in a couple of days. She'll be okay, Randi. I promise."

"Did Matthew leave?" She tried to sound like it didn't matter if he'd left her.

"He went to get me a soda. Jess didn't tell me you were dating someone."

Her relief that Matthew hadn't left was quickly replaced by anger. "That's because I'm not. Did he tell you that?" *Just wait until he comes back in here!* Just because she had a few stitches and accepted a ride home didn't mean they were a couple.

"No, I assumed you were. Why else would he be here?"

"Maybe he's just a nice guy who offered to help. That and he's a minister out to save all truck drivers from hell."

"That's different, then." Mike glanced at the clock on the wall. "I should be able to see her soon. They're supposed to call."

Randi peeked over her shoulder. A different volunteer had clocked in. "I need to call Dana and tell her what happened."

"Done."

"Did you call?"

"I did, but the police had already notified her. She said to check in when you get home."

Confused, Randi whirled around. Matthew stood holding a soda for Mike. "Mike told her you wouldn't need a ride." He handed the cup to Mike. "Did you want something, Randi?"

"No. I just want to see Jess." She rubbed the back of her neck.

A perky voice on the television behind her caught her attention. ". . .two truckers hospitalized after a drive-by shooting. Rare turtle gives birth. More in a moment."

Randi froze. "Is she talking about us?" The perky voice slowed and thickened, and overhead the lights dimmed.

Randi's knees ceased to exist. She slowly slid to the floor, vaguely aware of Matthew's hands around her waist. What did he think he was doing? *He'd better not...* Before she could finish the thought, the room tilted, spun, then faded to black.

৵

Matthew whispered her name. "Randi. Come back to us." He watched as her eyelids twitched. He desperately wanted them to open, revealing the most unusual eyes he'd ever seen, one blue and one green. He wanted to see them, to stare into their mesmerizing depths. He couldn't deny it; this woman had made it past his barriers. If he didn't distance himself soon, he might find he could never erase her from his mind.

"Matthew? What happened?" Her voice sounded weak and scared, a pale imitation of her normal one.

"You heard the newscast, and your body's defenses took over."

"What?"

"You fainted."

"Why didn't you say that?"

"I don't know. How do you feel now?" He cradled her head against his cheek, liking the feeling a little too much. He felt protective of her. She hadn't been out more than a minute, but she looked pale. It would be good to get out of here and take her home. Did she have someone to take care of her? He hadn't thought to ask.

The volunteer hovered nearby. "A nurse will be here in a second."

"No need, I'm fine." She sat up straighter and scooted away from Matthew.

"Maybe you are, but here she is, so let her check you out and we'll all feel better." The volunteer stepped back.

"Want to tell me what happened here?" The nurse wrapped her fingers around Randi's wrist and felt for her pulse.

"She heard the news about her partner being shot, and it

must have become real to her then, because she fainted. I caught her before she fell, though. She wasn't out very long."

"Your pulse is fine. If you feel faint again, make sure you sit down and lower your head to your knees." The nurse stepped back. "You can see your friend now if you feel strong enough."

"I'm ready."

Matthew watched her waver, as if she'd just vaulted off a boat and forgotten that land stood still. He hovered next to her. He wouldn't ask if he could go with her. She'd have to accept his being there, because she didn't have a choice. He had no intention of leaving her alone.

six

Randi closed her eyes and tried to rest against the seat of Matthew's truck, but she kept seeing Jess in that hospital bed, so pale, and no movement under that sheet. It was so unlike Jess to lie there like that. Even with over-the-counter allergy medications, she buzzed around the cab. With all her squirming, foot bouncing, and talking faster than a teenage girl with a new phone, she drove Randi crazy—so much so that Randi banned all medications from the cab. She'd rather listen to Jess's continual nose blowing.

Matthew grazed her arm with his fingertips, bringing her thoughts back to the front seat of his truck as he drove toward her home. "Are you thinking about Jess?"

She was so intent on memories, Matthew's touch surprised her. "How did you know?"

"It wasn't too hard to figure out. You haven't said much since before we left, when you made sure she was breathing."

"Guess that was kind of weird, wasn't it? Holding my hand under her nose to see if I could feel her breath?"

Matthew grinned then looked straight ahead as he maneuvered a curve in the road. "Can't say I've ever seen anyone do that."

"That's a safe answer." The pickup rattled; the diesel engine noise for once didn't soothe her. Randi stared out the window and wished she were home. He was driving her crazy, and they'd only been on the road for two hours. He was the worst kind of man. Hovering over her, asking if she needed anything. *Is the ride too rough? Do you want to stop for food? Are you too hot?* It was enough to make her wish she were back in the hospital. No one had fussed over her since she was six and had her appendix removed.

A soda can rolled from under the seat, striking against the heel of her boot. The truck reeked from fast-food bags and fries, pieces of which she found sticking out between the crack in the seat. The smell made her queasy. She pushed the can back with her toe. "Do you ever clean this thing?"

"Every other month. Ya think I need to do it more often?" Matthew gave her a sideways grin that turned to a frown when he saw her face. "Guess so. Sorry. I'd have cleaned if I'd known you were coming."

She didn't laugh at his feeble attempt at humor. She turned to face the open window, leaning forward to allow the wind to whip her hair. She'd lost the rubber band somewhere. It occurred to her that combing the tangles would not be pleasant. She gathered it into a clump with her hand and leaned even farther out the window to let the breeze cool her face. The miles rolled by, and she wondered what kind of person it took to shoot another, someone they didn't even know.

"What are you thinking about?" Matthew asked.

"Why there are evil people. Why does God allow them to live on the same planet as the good ones?" As soon as the words passed her lips, she thought about her brother. Did she think A.J. was evil? She could only think about the towheaded boy who'd played board games under the kitchen table with her. She thought about his laugh that bubbled like a spring from his chest. Emma laughed like him. Would she end up like her father?

"It's a sinful world, Randi. I don't know the answers. I do know God is giving everyone, good and bad, a chance to come to Him through His Son. Even the evil ones can change through His power." Matthew jiggled the air conditioner control as if it might miraculously fix itself.

"He's out there somewhere. Maybe even in one of the cars

we just passed." Randi watched weathered fence posts sail by the window.

"The police will catch him."

"I hope so. Before he shoots someone else." She hoped the news hadn't reported their names. It would be easier to explain what happened in person to her mom, when she showed up on her doorstep later tonight. Matthew insisted she go there, rather than home, or he wouldn't give her a ride. Did he think she would wake up screaming from a nightmare or something? "Why did you want me to go to my mom's?"

"Because you're taking pain pills, and you shouldn't be alone. I'd stay with you, but men don't stay with women they aren't married to."

"Maybe in your world." Her eyes darted to his left hand. "Are you married?"

"Not even close."

"Why? You do like women, right? Or is it because you're not allowed to get married?"

"I can marry. And yes, I do like women. A lot. It's just. . ."

"It's just what?"

He glanced in the side mirror then back at her. "I don't date a lot."

She cocked her head, squinted her eyes. Was he serious? "Who's the last person you dated?"

"Karen Landowny, in my senior year of college."

"So what happened?" Randi curled her foot beneath her, happy to be discussing something less serious, something that didn't involve her.

"She dumped me."

"Oh. I see." She tried not to smile at his morose tone.

"Are you assuming it's my fault she dumped me?"

"It wasn't?" Randi couldn't resist teasing. Surely he'd moved past a gone-wrong romance in the past. *But the same could apply to me.*

He hunkered over the steering wheel with a frown. "Great. Women stick together even when they've never met," Matthew grumbled under his breath, just loud enough for her to hear.

Apparently she'd misjudged his ability to move on with his life. He'd been nice to her, so she'd forgive his arrested development and show him some sympathy. "What happened?"

"Cows."

"What?" She whipped around and stared at him. Did he actually say "cows"?

"Cows. Lots of cows."

"I don't get it. What do cows have to do with dating?"

"My parents own a dairy farm."

"And?"

"Have you ever been to one? Driven by one?" He grimaced. Understanding dawned, and she surprised herself with a giggle like Emma's. "The smell kept you from dating?"

"My mom invited us to come back to the farm for a family celebration. Let's say Karen's reaction wasn't promising for a lifetime commitment. She told everyone my house smelled like pigs. And it doesn't smell like pigs; it smells like—"

"Cows."

His back became more erect, increasing his height. His head almost touched the roof of the truck. She stared at his profile. His jaw jutted noticeably. "Pigs smell more."

"Sure they do." Randi snickered.

seven

Matthew woke to sounds of the farm report on his radio. The first rays of sunlight had yet to streak their way into the Wyoming sky. But his room glowed from the dusk-to-dawn security light attached to the garage.

His dad would be expecting his help in the barn. Reluctantly, Matthew slid into his jeans and a T-shirt. He couldn't stay here much longer. True, he had his own place above the garage, but it was still his parents' home. He'd tried pastoring a small church after the seminary, but his heart wasn't in it. He longed to be out on the road, talking about the gospel to truckers who didn't get the chance to hear it. The longer he stayed, the easier it would be for his dream to slip away. He wasn't the kind of son who could live here and not see the need for his help on the farm. But he couldn't imagine milking cows day after day. And right now that's what his future seemed to hold. The only thing here to connect his hands to diesel fuel would be a tractor.

He pulled his Bible onto his lap. "Father, please start my life soon." Flipping it open to Psalms, he read a chapter then spent a few minutes in prayer. He asked for healing for Jess and Randi. Unwillingly, his mind evoked the picture of Randi's teasing smile and her blond hair whipping in the wind. Why did she haunt his thoughts, and now his prayers? No one else had found a way into his private life. Why her? He tried to push her image away. His work for the Lord was planned, and he didn't have time for a wife and family.

Whoa! Now I'm thinking about marriage? He shook his head to clear it and headed down the stairs. Maybe the cows would help get him centered on the plan he'd chosen.

Outside, the barn lights blazed through the windows. Once again his father had beaten him to the barn. When he walked through the huge wooden door, he found his dad, ball cap perched on his head and overalls already dusty, attaching teat cups to the cows' udders.

Matthew walked to the sink and washed his hands with disinfectant soap and water, then dried them with a paper towel. "Hey, Dad. Morning prayers took a little longer than usual today. Sorry."

"Never be sorry about talking to the Lord, Matthew. Talking to the Father is never wasted time." His father looked up and smiled. "I come down here and talk to Him while I'm getting the cows ready. Most mornings it's as if He's right here with me."

"Amazing, isn't it, Dad, how God can be with everyone at the same time?" Matthew flipped on the radio. "Might as well catch the weather while we're here."

"Yup. But I find it's more accurate if I stand outside and look for myself."

Matthew laughed. "I have to agree with you on that one. It seems the more sophisticated systems they have for predicting the weather, the more often they're wrong."

"Your uncle Danny already washed the teats. I'll get the rest of them hooked to the machine if you would turn the fans on high. Feels like it's going to be a scorcher today."

"Do we have any cows in the maternity ward?"

"No, maybe later this week. Go ahead and turn that fan on high, too. Helps to circulate the rest of the air." His father continued his task.

"These cows are spoiled. Their ancestors didn't have it this easy," Matthew said as he strode down the concrete walkway.

"And your ancestors didn't get as much milk from those cows, either," his dad yelled to him.

After he turned on and adjusted the fans, Matthew checked the hospital ward. The cow they had quarantined the night before seemed to be feeling better. He refilled the feed trough with the special food they saved for sick cows and gave her fresh water before leaving.

The sound of the milking machines made him feel like a kid again. If he closed his eyes, he could imagine his uncles standing in the barn talking to his dad, all of them red-cheeked from the sun, tattered ball caps on their heads. And lots of laughter. Now only Uncle Danny came to help. Uncle David had had a stroke and couldn't walk well, and Uncle Ray had retired and spent his time traveling around the country with a truck and fifth-wheel trailer.

"Woolgathering again?" His dad's voice intruded.

"Dad, when are you going to retire?" Matthew spun around to face him.

"Never. You retire, you might as well be dead. I like this life, and I'm not quitting until God takes me home." He patted the rump of a cow.

"But, Dad, how are you going to keep up with this if Uncle Danny retires?" Matthew leaned against the concrete wall.

"We've talked about that, and he isn't quitting, either." His dad removed his cap and ran his fingers through his sparse gray hair. " 'Course, we've also discussed the possibility you might grow tired of preaching to truck drivers and want to come back here. If that happens, the place is yours."

"Dad." Matthew hated disappointing his dad again. "Guess you and Uncle Danny are in for the long haul, then. I won't be changing my mind."

His dad nodded. "Okay, then, 'bout time to head back to the house."

"I wonder what Mom's making for breakfast."

"I requested some of her chocolate chip pancakes last night. Sure hope that's what she's doing." His father licked his lips. "Son, when you find someone to marry, you'd better make sure she can cook."

"Right. If she can't, I'll have to learn, or maybe move my family in with you." Matthew waited for his father's comeback and wasn't disappointed.

"Son, I didn't raise you to be a freeloader. You get a family. You take care of them."

"I will, Dad." Matthew slapped him on the back. "You've taught me well." He started to say more, but a nasal voice on the scratchy radio caught his ear.

". . .early this morning another truck driver was injured in a drive-by shooting. The suspect is still at large." *Randi. Has she heard about this yet? Maybe I should call and see if she's okay.*

His father removed his cap and ran his fingers through his thin gray hair. The look on his father's face said he'd heard the news also.

"I thought when you'd be driving trucks I wouldn't need to be concerned about your safety." His father's face looked pained. "Guess I was wrong about that."

"Let's go eat. They'll catch whoever is responsible. Think about all the truckers out there. The percentages of me being shot are pretty small, don't you think?" He reached out and punched his dad's arm with affection. "More likely I'll take to eating breakfast at night and wearing dirty clothes."

"Maybe. But don't mention this to your mother. She's a bit sensitive."

"Sure, Dad, I don't want her to worry that I might get hurt when I do get a job driving." Matthew swung his arm around his dad's shoulder and the two headed toward the house. Somewhere in a high tree, a mockingbird chattered, razzing him with a high-pitched whistle. Matthew clamped his lips tight and reached for the screen door, holding it for his father. *If I get a job, that is.*

eight

Since the shooting, Randi's mom had agreed to keep Emma. For a while. Randi still hoped her mom would decide it would be permanent.

Standing barefoot on her niece's bed, Randi carefully aimed a hammer at the shiny nail between her fingers then drove it into the wall. "That's the last one, Emma. Hand me your bear." Earlier she'd made loops to use as hooks and tied them to the ribbons strung like bowties around Emma's stuffed animals.

Emma handed her the polar bear. "That's Dusty."

"Hi, Dusty." Randi held the bear to her face. "I hope you like your new home." With great care she hung the bear on the nail. She sank back onto the bed, eyeing her craftsmanship with skepticism. "What do you think?"

Emma stood at the foot of the bed and tipped her head one way, then the other. "They aren't even."

"You're right, I didn't get them all at the same height. Does that bother you?"

"No. But they aren't even."

Randi looked at the wall again and understood. The bed wasn't centered under the animals, leaving enough space to put one more animal. If Emma had another one. . .but she didn't. She didn't have much of anything. A. J.'s house and its contents were seized when he was arrested. Social services had packed a suitcase and let Emma pick a few things to bring with her. The small dresser top held three books and a generic fashion doll whose hair frizzed as if she'd been vacationing in the tropics. The room looked empty. Maybe Randi could fix this one problem. "Wait right here."

She headed for the kitchen, knowing she would find her mom sitting at the table working a crossword puzzle. "Do you still have that box of stuff from when I was a kid?"

"Look in the top of the front closet. I almost tossed it out a month ago. They were collecting for the church yard sale. I didn't think you wanted it, since you'd left it here for so long. But I thought I should ask first."

"I don't—didn't want it. But I think there might be a few treasures Emma might like."

She found the box on the top shelf, pushed into the corner. It wasn't a lot of stuff, but maybe it would be enough for now. She carried it into Emma's new room.

"What's in there?" Emma asked.

"I'm not sure. Want to help me look?" Randi plopped the box on the floor and hunkered down next to it. She sat down and patted the spot next to her. "Well?"

Emma looked at her warily for a moment. "Okay."

Randi pulled the flap open. On top there was tissue paper. She pulled it out. Underneath was what she had been looking for. *Tally.* He was in perfect condition. She stroked his golden fur then handed him to Emma. "He used to be mine, but I'd like for you to have him."

"What's his name?"

"Tally. But I think he wouldn't mind if you wanted to call him something else."

Emma held the dog in front of her, turning and twisting him. "I think Tally is a good name. Who gave him to you?"

Randi's memory jumped to Christmas morning. Her father had left them that summer and she'd never heard from him again. Eventually Mom had said he'd found someone else to love. The spindly tree leaned crookedly in the corner, surrounded by silver and gold packages her mom hadn't bought—beautifully wrapped packages. Later she learned they were brought by their church. Inside one of them was the stuffed cocker spaniel she named Tally. She decided TV Dad had sent him to her secretly. It had been a long time since she'd thought of him. She and A.J. had made him up after watching *The Cosby Show.* They wanted to have a dad like Cliff Huxtable and decided to pretend they did and named him TV Dad. "I don't know, Emma. He was under our Christmas tree one year."

"Can we hang him, too?"

"Sure, we just need another safety pin. Can you get me one?"

Emma jumped up from the floor. "I'll get one from Grandma. I'll be right back."

Randi grinned when she realized Emma held Tally tightly as she left the room. She poked around in the box, wondering what else she had considered a treasure once upon a time. She heard the phone ring in the background and hoped it would be Emma's friend. She hadn't called since Emma moved.

"Aunt Randi?" Emma held the phone out to her. "It's for you. Some man."

Mike? Did something go wrong with Jess? Her heart rate increased. She leaped from the floor, forgetting the box of memories and grabbing the phone from Emma. "Mike?"

"No, Matthew."

Matthew? Her mind went blank for a split moment before realization brought a rush of heat to her face. She scrunched her brows. "Hi."

"I tried your cell phone, but you didn't answer. I thought you might be at your mom's. I wondered if you would like to have dinner tonight."

"With you?"

"Well, I suppose I could arrange for you to have dinner with someone else if you want, but yeah, I guess I hoped you'd go with me." The teasing tone in his voice returned the heat to her cheeks. "I really want to see for myself that you're okay. I've been looking for you on the road."

"I haven't gone back to work yet. Not until next week." She glanced up to see Emma watching intently. "I have plans for tonight, but if you don't mind if I bring someone along—"

"Sure. Do you want to meet me, then? I thought I'd take you—we could meet at Bill's Grill. Do you know where that is?"

"Around six?"

"That works for me. I'll see you and. . ."

She let the question hang. Did she detect a jealous tone in his voice? "We'll be there." She pushed the END button a little too quickly. She blinked at Emma.

"Who was that, Aunt Randi?" Emma raked her fingers through the fur on the cocker spaniel's ear.

"The man you and I are having dinner with tonight."

"We're going on a date?" A grin stretched across Emma's face. Her eyes widened. "Do you love him?"

Randi smiled, painfully aware that her cheeks were on fire. "No, he's a friend." She chewed on her lip and tossed the phone onto the bed. At least she hoped he was just a friend. Or did he want to be more? Worse yet, why didn't she know how she felt about that? And why had she said "friend" instead of "pastor"?

⁂

Matthew slammed the door and stomped down the stairs of his apartment. Who was Randi bringing? She'd said she wasn't dating. He fished the keys to his truck out of his pocket and got in, ramming them into the ignition. No, she said there wasn't anyone to call. Wasn't that the same thing? She obviously had someone in her life, and he didn't like the idea. Not one bit. Well, at least tonight he would meet the competition. *If there even is competition!* No! He just wanted to make sure she was okay, that's all. After all, that's what a pastor did, or a big brother. Right? Yeah. A pastor or big brother. But something way down deep in his heart told him he didn't want to be either of those to Randi.

nine

Randi's fingers trembled as she pushed the lock button for her pickup. The ride to the restaurant had made her long for the quiet of the road. Emma's shotgun questions had only made her more aware of Matthew as an eligible male, not a pastor. What if he was interested in her, not just her soul? Could she handle that? Did she want to drive down that road?

Emma stretched her arms wide and twirled on the sidewalk. "Do you think our date is here yet?"

"It's not a date, Emma," Randi explained one more time. "A date picks you up at your house and takes you in his car. He doesn't meet you at the restaurant, at the mall, or at the movies."

"And Pastor Carter isn't taking us. We're taking us. So it's not a date." Emma's head bobbed in agreement with Randi. "But why did we have to change clothes and curl our hair?"

"Because we're girls, and we like to look nice for us." Randi held out her hand. "Ready?"

Emma slid her hand into Randi's. "Is he cute?"

"Emma. It's not a—"

"Date. I know, but is he?"

"He is." Great. That would just add more stress to this outing. But she couldn't lie. Emma could see for herself that Matthew. . . Well, she wasn't going to finish that thought.

They pushed through the glass doors, and the smell of grilled hamburgers and onions wafted through the air. A country song ricocheted against the walls. Bill's Grill boasted ten tables. Matthew wasn't at any of them. *Definitely not a date if he isn't already waiting.* The disappointment flowed through her, but she brushed the feeling away and attributed it to Emma's pestering.

"Can we sit over there?" Emma pointed to the stainless steel bar with tomato red tractor seat stools.

"I think a table might be better. If Matthew's been driving a lot, he'll want to have someplace to rest his back." Randi knew that from experience. She never sat on stools after a long drive unless there wasn't anything else available. Someone touched her shoulder, and she spun around. "Matthew."

"You're right. I'd rather sit at a table." He wore a huge grin.

"What are you so happy about?" Something about that grin made her think he was more than just happy to see her. But what?

"I'm Emma. Are you our date?"

Randi felt the color start to rise in her face. "Emma."

"Sorry, Aunt Randi. I know he's not a date because he didn't pick us up."

"I'll be your date, Miss Emma, if you like."

Matthew beamed, positively beamed. Could he like the idea of them dating? Randi didn't know what to do with the feelings jumping around inside her.

"If he's not your date, can he be my date, Aunt Randi?"

The end of this outing couldn't come soon enough for Randi. She should have left the girl at home with her grand-mother. Then Emma looked at her with hope spilling from her face. She was probably the only eight-year-old in this town to date a pastor. Her stories at school would be stupendous. "Emma."

"Please, just this once, couldn't we say it's a date?"

The kid had been through a lot. She might as well have a bright spot in her day. Randi felt her resolve melting. "Just this once."

"You may get us a table." Emma tipped her chin and stared

at Matthew. "And you can sit next to me."

Matthew blinked in surprise. Emma had Randi's eyes, and Matthew must have noticed. He looked back at Randi.

Reading his expression, Randi said, "Almost the same. They're reversed."

"Fascinating family trait."

"On the playground it's anything but that."

Emma tugged on Matthew's hand and pointed. "That table by the window. Can we sit there?"

"Looks like a perfect place for my pretty date. Why don't you lead the way?"

Emma flashed him a grin. "Okay!" She raced across the room as if there were others rushing for the prime spot in the diner. In seconds she had the menu in front of her.

Matthew pulled out a chair next to Emma, across from Randi.

Randi plucked a laminated menu from the silver prongs that held it tight between the mustard and ketchup. After a moment, she made her choice. "Emma, what do you want?"

"I don't know yet." Emma slid her finger along the words on the menu. She looked at Randi wide-eyed. "What can I have?"

Matthew leaned over and whispered into Emma's ear. She giggled.

"I get to have a chocolate shake, and we're going bowling at Ten Pin Bowl-a-Rama after!" Emma bounced in her seat.

Randi fumed and focused her best imitation of her mother's "I'm not pleased" look at Matthew. She'd agreed to dinner, nothing else. Matthew should have asked her before telling Emma. She'd march right out of here after dinner if Emma wasn't positively glowing with happiness. If A.J. hadn't been an irresponsible parent, she wouldn't be in this situation. At times like this she could barely contain her anger at her brother.

Bowling balls rumbled down the lanes next to him as Matthew finished typing their names into the automatic scoreboard. "Emma, you're up first."

Emma stood looking at him, holding the bright pink ball she'd picked out of the rack. She watched the bowler in the next lane. When his ball left his hand, she copied his hand movement. He threw his ball. She didn't throw hers. She turned slightly and watched a bowler on the other side.

"Has she ever bowled?" he asked Randi.

She gave a slight shake of her head. "I doubt it. Her home life hasn't been the greatest."

"Should I help her?"

"Maybe. No, wait, she's trying."

Emma's ball loped down the lane and into the gutter with a plop. She walked back with her head low, wiping tears with her sleeve. "This is a stupid game. Can we go home?"

Matthew felt at a loss. He looked at Randi for help. She didn't offer any, shrugging her shoulders as if to say, "You wanted to take her bowling. It's your problem to fix." He straightened his back.

"Emma. You're doing it just right. We're playing crazy bowl."

Both of them looked at him as if he'd lost his mind. "Yeah, it's a cool way to bowl because each round you have to do something different. My grandmother is a bowler. In Illinois they play this game for fun. This frame you have to get a gutter ball. Emma, for a beginner you're really good."

He grabbed his ball, walked to the alley, and slung it down the lane. All ten pins fell over. He pasted a frown on his face before turning around.

"See, Emma? It's not easy to get a gutter ball. Randi, you're up."

As she walked by, he stopped her and whispered, "I'll be right back. I'm going to the front desk. I'm hoping they will override the automatic scoring for me and maybe have a sheet of crazy bowl ideas."

He returned waving a piece of lined yellow paper. "They have a rock 'n' roll night that sounds like fun. They have music, strobe lights, and the pins light up, but they haven't heard of crazy bowl. I explained it to the manager, though, and he helped me come up with some ideas. This is going to be so much fun. Emma, you're up, and this time you have to sit on the floor with the ball between your legs and push it with your hands. Try for the middle, because if you knock pins down, it counts."

Emma bounced from the orange plastic seat and headed for the alley with her ball.

"So are you dating anyone?"

Smooth, Carter. You might have led up to that.

She shrugged her shoulder. "Not unless you count that speed-dating thing Jess made me do. That miserable night an entire conveyer belt of men passed by, and I let them keep going."

"Are you going to watch me?" Emma stood at the ball return, tapping her foot.

"We're watching!" Matthew was thankful for her interruption. He'd asked a question and gotten an answer he didn't know what to do with.

Emma held the ball to her chest as she walked to the beginning of the lane. She sat on the floor and placed the ball between her outstretched legs, then gave it a mighty shove. The ball sailed into the pins, knocking down five. Emma jumped up, clapped her hands over her head, and spun in a circle celebrating her success. "I did it! This is fun! What's next?"

"Standing on your left leg." Randi read from the paper. "And the next one—" She laid the paper on the table next to the uneaten nachos.

"Is what, Aunt Randi?"

"I think it's time to go home. Grandma is probably waiting for us to come home and watch that movie she rented." Randi sat on the chair and started to untie her bowling shoe.

Matthew picked up the paper, wondering what caused her sudden change of interest. *"Place your hands over the next player's eyes and guide him with words."* So she didn't want him touching her? Or was it whispering into her ear she objected to?

"Afraid of me?"

"No—no. I thought maybe we'd been gone too long, taking up too much of your time."

"I'm fine. I've already paid for the game. We might as well finish." He grinned, watching emotions race across her face. "For Emma."

"Please, Aunt Randi. This is fun."

Randi retied her shoe. "Fine. Let's just get this done." She slammed her foot down on the concrete floor. "And I'll repay you later."

Matthew watched her stomp off, enjoying her feisty attitude.

ten

As the sun fell lower in the western sky, Randi consulted the truck stop guide that lay on the seat next to her. She'd driven seven hours today and needed a place to sleep soon. The last rest stop she passed was already filled, in every legal and creative parking space. No sane driver wanted to go through Cheyenne during rush hour, but it didn't look as though she'd have a choice.

She slapped the book shut. If she'd been able to get out of the last place on time—but that meant they would have had to let her unload at her scheduled time. That never happened. She'd drive hard and fast to make it on time, and they'd make her wait every time. It didn't matter who she delivered to, either. Produce, meat, or rock, they all made her wait. And that cost her in mileage, which translated into a smaller paycheck.

If she hadn't overslept. . .

Dana called her on the cell phone. As soon as she realized she'd woken Randi, she started yelling. Randi couldn't blame her, since it wasn't the first time since she'd returned to work; more like the third in a week. Driving alone was harder than she had imagined. True, she and Jess sometimes ran late, but not like this. She knew she couldn't afford to run late again, at least not for a while. Her job could be in jeopardy.

The white lines dashed by, and her mind drifted to the evening with Matthew two weeks ago. Randi wanted to think of anything besides Matthew, his hands covering her eyes, his quiet voice. Just thinking about his breath on her ear sent her heart into a panic. She couldn't allow him to get to her; she couldn't allow him into her life. She'd made her choice. "Stand alone—let no man join me" was her mantra. But she couldn't help but wonder a little what it would be like to be his wife.

She grabbed a cup from the cup holder and dumped crushed ice into her mouth. The cold helped perk her sagging energy. Had Matthew found a company to drive for yet? She couldn't seem to keep him out of her thoughts. Frustrated, she chomped on the ice and blamed Jess. If she would come back to work, there would be someone to distract her. They could talk about Jess's marriage plans.

She still hadn't told Randi about getting engaged, and Mike hadn't placed a ring on Jess's finger. Unless she didn't wear it when Randi came over? No. Jess wouldn't hide a diamond; more like her to flaunt it. Randi hadn't stayed long enough for a long conversation, but now that she thought about it, Jess didn't even mention Mike. That couldn't be good. Jess had better not mess up this relationship. If Randi had reservations before, they'd disappeared after Jess was shot. That man was by Jess's side until he took her home. Now that was the kind of husband Randi wanted, or would want if she were looking for one.

But she wasn't.

Matthew seemed to be good with children, too. At least Emma thought so. He would be a good father figure for Emma. She wouldn't stop talking about him on the way home that night. Maybe he would call them again.

Stop! This has to end. Driving alone gave a person too much time to think about future possibilities. And she didn't want to include him.

She drummed on the steering wheel with her thumb. *What else could I think about?* Not her mom. This morning when Randi called, she'd received an earful of complaints. Her mom couldn't go to the Ladies' Society because Emma needed to go to the library after school. To hear Mom, you would think she'd missed the doorway to heaven by not attending the meeting with that gaggle of gossiping women.

Still, Randi felt guilty. Her earlier promise to relieve her mom didn't seem like much if she couldn't do it. But wasn't that enough proof that she couldn't have Emma living with her? Where would Emma go for the two to three weeks Randi sometimes had to be on the road? Randi hadn't seen her own bed for days. That wouldn't be a life for a kid. Emma deserved someone involved in her life every day. The red light on the Qualcomm lit. She groaned. Jess called it the wannabe computer. The light meant dispatch had a message for her. Probably a change she didn't want to know about. It would have to wait until she found a safe place to pull over. The brake lights on the car in front of her came on, causing her to downshift. Instead of slowing, the motor raced. Randi's heart thudded. She pumped the clutch again and tried to shift lower. The engine continued racing. *The clutch.* No doubt about it, the thing was slipping and getting hotter the longer she stayed on the road. Her choice of driving farther expired as she pulled the rig to the side of the road. Dana would not be happy to hear from her.

⁂

After jiggling the diesel fuel nozzle back into its slot, Matthew screwed the cap onto the tank then climbed into the cab and moved his truck forward, freeing the space for the driver waiting behind him to fuel. Leaving the door open, he swung the pickup into a parking spot at the back of the building, avoiding the front entrance where the tourists entered. He reached down to the floorboard on the passenger side and scooped up a small duffel bag holding a change of clothes. His arms felt crystallized with dried sweat. He imagined his stench had to be as bad as the farm's. He hated to spend the last few dollars he had on a shower, but if he didn't, he wouldn't get one for at least another day. It was only July, but he kept bugging God to send him a job with an air-conditioned truck. He knew it was just a matter of time—God's time, not his—but he wished he could speed up God.

He headed inside to pay, glancing down at the pavement in time to avoid stepping on a moist mound of chewing tobacco. Inside, the cool air washed over him, refreshing him like a summer romp in the hose.

At the counter he pulled his wallet from his back pocket. "How long until a shower's available?" Once again he bemoaned the fact that he was driving his own truck and not a big rig. He would have to pay for a shower because he didn't have enough fueling credits for a free one.

The clerk popped her gum. "Um, 'bout fifteen minutes."

"I'd like to buy time in one, then." He handed over his credit card to pay, wondering what the IRS thought about deductions for showers.

She ran his card through the machine and waited for him to sign. Transaction completed, she reached under the counter and handed him a small bar of wrapped soap, a towel, and a wash rag. "Number 153."

"Thanks." He wandered to the drivers' lounge to wait for his number to be called and stopped inside the doorway. It seemed to be empty except for one bearded driver smoking in the back. Then he noticed her. Randi was curled up against the wall in a booth, her blond hair glimmering like gold against the backdrop of the dark blue wall. Her arms were tightly wrapped against her chest. Both eyes were closed, and she seemed to be sleeping.

"What are you looking at, Preacher Boy? Haven't you seen a stranded trucker before?" Her eyelids barely lifted.

He slid into the booth across from her. "How's the padded-vinyl mattress?" He gestured at the back of the booth.

"Real funny. I'm stuck here. The clutch burned out and they've got it in the shop; no clutch, no air-conditioning."

"How long you been here?"

"Couple of hours."

"Rough when you can't stay in your truck. Have you eaten?"

She pointed at the empty glass in front of her. "A diet cola and a chocolate bar."

He didn't think that qualified as dinner but refrained from saying it. "Where you headed?"

"Sioux Falls. I was supposed to be going to Jackson, but they Qualcommed me with the change. I've been stalling my call home. This is going to fry my mom. Emma's going to be disappointed, too, since this will put me out further from coming home."

The dark circles under her eyes alarmed him. She must be driving more hours than she was allowed. "Been gone long?"

"Couple of days. I thought I'd be home tomorrow night." She slid her legs along the length of the booth. "Are you still dragging boats behind you?"

He nodded. "Still waiting. How's Jess?"

"She's better. She's only taking the pain pills at night." She tilted her head back against the wall and closed her eyes.

Matthew wanted to tell her to go home, crawl into bed, take a bath—anything that would be good for her. He couldn't. He didn't have that right. Besides, she couldn't do any of those things tonight. Or could she?

He twisted the shower ticket in his hand. He hated to give it up, but it felt like the right thing to do. "Randi?"

"Mmm?" She didn't open her eyes.

"I just realized I can't wait for the shower to be free." He pushed the ticket across the table.

She picked it up. "You have to use it or you lose it."

"That's just it. I have to give it up. Why don't you take it?" He hoped she would. If she was getting back in a rig tonight, she needed something to waken her. He plopped the towel and soap on the table. "So?"

Tears welled in her eyes. He hadn't meant to make her cry. He wanted to make her smile. And then she did, and he felt the room brighten.

"Matthew. That is the nicest thing anyone has done for me in a long time." She reached across the table and touched his hand. "Are you sure you don't have time to use it yourself?"

He gave her hand a gentle squeeze. "I want you to have it. I've got to head back tonight." Then he let go. He felt as if he'd lost a piece of himself. Not only did he have to give up holding her hand, but he'd have to leave now, or she'd know he'd given it to her out of kindness. And he had a hunch she'd throw it back in his face if she knew. She was that type, a woman who didn't accept help from anyone. Why was it so difficult to get close to this woman?

❧

Perplexed, Randi watched Matthew's retreating back. He'd given her his shower. Why? Did he think she needed one? Or that she couldn't get one herself? Still, since she was stuck here and had it in her hand, why not? The idea of warm water and fresh clothes sounded heavenly to her.

She reached to the floor and hauled her backpack to her lap. She checked the small bag of toiletries she carried; she had enough shampoo and shower gel. She never used the soap they handed out at the counter. If she didn't know better, she would think it was lye soap, just packaged pretty, to kill off whatever crawled around in those bathrooms.

"Shower 153 now ready. One-fifty-three now ready."

Sliding across the booth, she realized she hadn't thanked Matthew for the shower, and then realized there were a lot of things she should have thanked him for already.

eleven

Randi stared across the metal desk at her boss, Dana Foster. "How can you assign a man to drive with me? The only reason I work here is because they don't make me drive with a male."

"You don't need to shout. This isn't personal, Randi. It's what needs to be done and what my boss wants done. I don't have the power to override his decision. What do you need to make this work?" She straightened the papers in front of her into a neat pile and then fanned them out.

"It won't work. I *need* to not have a man assigned to drive with me. I can drive alone until Jess gets back." Randi struggled to keep the anger out of her voice.

"Not an option, Davis. You gave that a try, and you can't do it. You oversleep and deliver late. You're lucky I suggested you for this job instead of letting you go."

"I won't make enough money if I can't drive long hauls." She twisted her hands together as she pleaded with Dana.

"You won't make as much, but the company is willing to compensate for some loss in pay."

At the word "compensate," Randi narrowed her eyes. "Why so generous?"

"They considered you would be supervising the new driver."

"A trainee? You're assigning me a novice?"

"He's a driver, but he hasn't had a lot of time in a rig. He's also a minister. He came to the company with a unique idea of combining an over-the-road ministry with the company. The owner became a Christian recently, and since then he's been checking out the Truckers for Christ program. He

65

wants to do something for his drivers, if they want to attend some kind of service."

Randi collapsed into the wooden chair in front of Dana's desk. "Matthew Carter."

"You know him, then?"

"Yeah, he brought me home from the hospital." *And charmed my niece and gave me his shower.* "So the only way to keep my job is accepting a man into my cab?" Randi stood and paced in front of the desk, the heels of her boots clapping against the tiled floor. She stopped at the bookshelf, plucked a yellowed leaf from a philodendron plant, and carried it to the trash can. She released it from her fingers and watched it float onto a brown apple slice.

"He's not just a man. Think of him as a pastor. Or you can opt to work for another company, take unpaid leave until Jess returns, or elect to take another woman as a permanent partner. Your choice. So what's it going to be?"

"Those aren't options I can consider." She watched Dana's upper lip curve downward.

Dana tapped a pencil on the desktop. Randi heard irritation in those taps; they weren't her usual "One, two, three, move" taps. These sounded more like stiletto heels running over cobblestones.

"That's life. I have to know right now what you're going to do. You're scheduled to meet him Monday morning. All right? It won't be that bad, Randi. It's only for a few weeks until Jess comes back. Think how good this will look on your record when Johnson reads it at review time." The wheels on Dana's chair screeched as she pushed away from the desk.

Randi stared at her, willing her to change her mind. Silence bounced back, filling the space in the room. "I guess I'll do it. But I don't like it."

"So noted. But I won't write the last part on your file." Dana's laugh cracked into a hacking dry cough.

"Give up those cigarettes yet?" Randi had been trying to get her to quit since Dana had a mild heart attack a year ago.

"I'm trying. It isn't easy. I've been smoking since I was eleven, and after this discussion I could use one."

"Look, don't blame your addiction on me. There are things out there to help you quit. You"—Randi shot Dana her best evil grin—"have to make a choice. I don't want to drive with Matthew, and you don't seem to appreciate fresh air. Let's make a deal. You have six weeks, the same six I have to ride with Matthew. Six weeks of me not calling you to complain."

"And if I don't quit?"

Randi thought about it for a moment. What could bother Dana enough to make her think twice about lighting a cigarette?

"Jess and I don't drive weekends for a month."

"A four-weekend month, not a five."

"Deal. Six weeks, and your office better not smell like cigarettes." She held out her hand to seal the deal.

Back in her truck, she wished she hadn't promised to keep driving. But she had. Knowing she didn't have a choice made it harder to accept being told who was going to ride in her cab. If she had enough money, she'd become an owner-operator. She needed and wanted her own truck—not a man to share it with.

A man, any man, would not—no, could not—ever be allowed into her life again.

❧

Monday morning, Randi arrived an hour early at the Round the Clock shipping yard. After checking in with Dana, she made arrangements for Dana to drop Matthew at the truck stop so she could get breakfast. Randi picked up the truck and headed down the street.

Pushing open the heavy doors of the diner, she inhaled the scent of fresh-brewed coffee.

"Yum, just what I need." She headed for the counter.

"Hey, Randi."

Randi turned and flashed a smile at the girl behind the gift shop cash register. "Hi yourself, Brenda. How's the baby?"

"Hard to leave, she's so precious."

Randi didn't like the tired lines etched across her friend's face. "Are you thinking about staying home instead of working?"

"I'd like to, just to get some rest if nothing else. Soon Angela should be sleeping all night. That will help." Brenda sighed. "Staying home just isn't possible being a single mother. I have to bring home the paycheck. No one else will."

"Marry a rich trucker." Randi smiled, waiting for Brenda to laugh.

Brenda didn't fail her. When the laughter quit, she said, "There aren't any rich truckers, but I'll get married the day after you say 'I do.' From what I've experienced, there are only two kinds of men out there: 'Love 'em and leave 'em,' or 'Once a cheat, always a cheat.'"

"Guess we'll both be on our own and in charge of our own futures."

"Fine with me." Brenda squirted window cleaner on the glass counter and wiped it with a paper towel. "Seems to me we're the only ones who really know what we need to be happy, anyway."

"Could be, Brenda." Randi's stomach growled. "I'll catch you later. My stomach is calling for Terry's early bird special."

Randi walked into the dining area and headed straight for the counter. She patted the puffy yellow vinyl seat on the stool as if in greeting. She thought of it as her stool, her little spot of sunshine. She placed her foot on the chrome footrest, hopped on, and gave herself a spin, stopping with her hands on the gray granite Formica counter.

"Why do you always do that, Randi?" A man in a white

apron and cap gave her a gap-toothed smile.

"Terry, I can't help it. If I don't spin first, it's like my day hasn't started off right. And today I have to make sure it takes off in the right direction." Randi looked over her shoulder and frowned.

"What evil thing are you expecting to walk through that door?" Terry leaned his elbows on the counter and peered into her face.

"A new partner. I don't like sharing a cab with someone new. The company won't let me drive alone, and since Jess is on disability, I don't have a choice."

"What's her name?"

"It's not a she. It's a he." Not liking the gleam in Terry's eyes, Randi decided to switch the subject, fast. "Besides, turning on the bar stool is just a fun thing to do. Not like the weird things you do. Like wearing Halloween and Christmas socks and hanging streamers from your antenna to celebrate National Pig Day. So don't pretend I'm strange."

"Humph." Terry shrugged his shoulders. "At least I do exciting things. Besides, Pig Day is a big deal if your brother raises them. Tell me, when was the last time you did anything to make your blood race?"

"Every time I order your special blend hot chocolate, my blood runs hot and fast." Randi crossed her hands across her chest, tilted her head, and batted her eyes at him. "One glance at that mile-high whipped cream and I think I just might die completely satisfied."

"Need a life. You need a life." Terry shook his head. "What do you want this morning?"

"Scrambled eggs, biscuits, and to perk up my life—hot chocolate instead of coffee. Toss some colored sprinkles on the whipped cream." Randi grinned at his surprised frown. "Just needing a bit of excitement this morning, Terry."

"Need a life. You need to marry a nice man, settle down,

and have a few kids," Terry mumbled as he headed to the kitchen.

Randi stood on the bar stool rungs and hung over the counter, yelling as Terry disappeared into the kitchen, "I heard that! I have a fine life, thank you very much."

At least it was fine, up 'til now.

&

Matthew Carter crossed over the threshold of PJ's Truck Emporium. He stood in the gift shop, thanking God. He'd followed his dream. And now he was here, standing in an aisle surrounded by snakes in fake peanut cans, glass piggy banks, and souvenir spoons crested with cowboys riding broncos. He'd made it, and it felt good.

He dropped his backpack on the black-and-white tile floor and looked for someone who could point out the driver he would be working with.

"Can I help you?"

Matthew turned. A woman in a uniform the color of butterscotch, topped with a white apron, peeked over the top of the cash register. She was almost hidden behind clear plastic containers of combs, novelty pens, and dollar items.

"I need to page R. Davis. Can you do that?"

"Sure. What do you need Davis for?" She gave him a cool stare and smacked her gum.

"He's my new partner. We're riding together for a while."

"Sure thing, honey." Her face broke into a wide smile as she pulled a shiny microphone toward her, flicking it on with her finger then tapping it a few times. "Davis, Randi Davis. Please come to the gift shop. Someone is here to see you."

Did she say Randi? Matthew's heart beat faster. Could it be his Randi? He swung around in time to see Randi pull a wad of money out of her jeans pocket. Her painted nails flashed as she sorted through the green then flipped some dollar bills onto the counter. Intrigued, he watched her take a sip of some awful-looking frothy concoction. She brushed her long hair behind her ears and walked toward him.

The cashier behind him giggled.

Glancing over his shoulder, Matthew looked back at her. He turned around again and caught the container of ink pens with his hand, knocking it sideways. Pens rolled across the counter and clattered onto the tile floor.

Grumbling in his embarrassment, Matthew bent down to pick them up.

"I hope you can control a rig better than your hands." Randi's soft voice, like spun honey, graced his ears.

Matthew looked up, a long way up, past long, jean-clad legs. A woman's legs. The woman who wouldn't stay out of his mind stood before him. His old inability to talk to women resurfaced as he stood. "It's you," he sputtered.

"Sure is. Are you ready to pull out?"

"I thought I'd be riding with a man. R. Davis."

She smirked. Her full lips glistened, and he caught the scent of peaches. If he kissed her, would she taste like a fresh peach? He mentally shook himself.

"This is R. Davis, woman driver." She pointed at her chest. "If you don't want to ride with me, then don't. You can call the company, and they'll tell you I'm it or nothing."

Matthew could see she was a woman. Pure woman. The blue plaid shirt she wore over a white T-shirt made her eyes sparkle. The gold locket nestled in the hollow of her neck enticed him to run his fingers under it. She brought feelings, good ones, racing through his body. Trouble, definitely trouble. God was going to have to take control of this situation, fast.

"I thought your last name was Bell." At least that was what they'd printed on her plastic armband in the emergency room.

"It is, but I use Davis."

"Why Davis?"

"Maybe I'll tell you sometime, but not now."

"I'll ride along to the next stop. Maybe by then we can get this straightened out." Matthew tossed his backpack over his shoulder and made a mental note to retrieve his Bible before pulling out of the lot. He needed God's guidance on this one. He followed Randi to the truck, trying not to watch her walk. He shook his head in bewilderment. *What could God be thinking?*

Close to the cab, Randi yelled behind her, "Don't even think about asking to drive my truck, Preacher Boy."

Matthew groaned inside. Yes, sir, trouble in more ways than one. He'd have to do some hard time on his knees trying to find a way to be grateful to God for throwing him into the hot seat. He'd almost been able to quit thinking about her every hour of the day, and now this. He looked up to see Randi staring at him. Her stance told him she was ready to battle for her right to drive.

"You have a look that says you could take on a whole football team without protective gear." Matthew smiled. "My sister looks like that when she's mad."

"My brother taught me everything I need to survive in a man's world."

"That explains why you drive a truck, I suppose," Matthew murmured.

"Excuse me?" Randi pulled her sunglasses from the V-neck of her T-shirt and slipped them on. "I didn't catch that."

"Nothing important." Matthew thought better of repeating himself. No need to get in an argument when he wasn't planning to stick around long enough to finish it. He didn't need a woman in his life, especially this one. She had already become a distraction to him. Getting to know her and Emma had been a huge mistake, because the two of them, with their unusual eyes, had him bewitched.

Matthew ran his hand over the fender of the truck. "This is nice rig."

"It's a good company to work for. They take care of their drivers."

"What are we hauling?"

Randi's eyebrows rose at his question. Maybe she didn't consider him a part of the "we." *She may be beautiful, Carter, but she has a vicious attitude toward you.* Maybe this was how God planned to keep him safe.

"We. . ."

Matthew noticed she stressed that word.

"Are hauling concrete fountains."

Matthew stood back and admired the cobalt blue mid-rise rig for a moment. "Round the Clock Trucking. Interesting name, but it does say it all, doesn't it?"

"Sounds like an adventure, doesn't it? We'll revisit that thought in a few weeks, since we won't be taking any long hauls. Toss your stuff in back, and we'll walk through the pre-trip together."

He frowned. Long hauls were his real dream, not day trips.

twelve

A minivan passed the truck. In the back, two small children frantically motioned. Randi couldn't resist the small arms trying to get her to blow the horn. "Carter, watch this."

The air horn blasted, and the kids collapsed in laughter.

"That looked like fun. Did they try long?" Matthew asked.

"No. I gave in quick." She loved driving a truck, almost being responsible only for herself. She and Jess shared that feeling, the one of being the biggest on the road and savoring the savage power that flowed through the wheel. Would Matthew Carter feel the same way?

Randi glanced at her new partner. She wouldn't know he was a preacher boy if she didn't know him. He didn't dress like any preacher she'd ever met. No white shirt with a dark tie around his neck, dress pants, and shiny loafers. This preacher boy wore nice-fitting jeans and a T-shirt that hinted at muscles made for a woman's hand to caress. For a moment she thought about touching his dark, wavy hair, and then her glance fell on the Bible on his lap.

"Are you going to read that thing all the way to Buffalo?"

Matthew turned a page before answering her. "No, I was just thinking about my first sermon."

Proved me wrong. He's a pastor hiding in civilian clothes, all right. "What's it going to be about?"

"Temptation, I think." Matthew stretched his arms over his head. "Sure you don't want me to take a turn at the wheel?"

Randi glared at him. "No. Why would I?"

"Because you might want to look at the fields of corn and the occasional cow we pass?"

"Not a snowball's chance in—never mind." Randi cringed inside. She didn't talk like the stereotypical trucker; just because it was the job she'd chosen didn't mean she had to play the part. But this man was enough to exasperate anyone. Still, she regretted almost making a slip.

"You were going to say 'hell'? I think that's an appropriate phrase. Snowballs will not survive in hell. In fact, the way I understand it, nothing we love and enjoy will survive in hell."

"Look, I wasn't asking for a sermon." Randi reached over and popped in a CD. Lyle Lovett bellowed, cutting off any conversation.

Matthew reached over and turned down the volume. "Sorry, it hurts my ears. Do you have anything softer? Classical, maybe?"

"None. Everything I have is blues or country, and loud is how I like it." This didn't make things any easier. If Carter didn't like the same kind of music, this *would* be a long haul. The worst part was, she couldn't even complain to Dana.

"Why do you like the blues?"

"I don't know. I think because it gets down into your soul and speaks to the pain that engulfs your heart." Randi flipped on the left turn signal, shifted, and changed lanes.

He pulled out a package of gum and offered her a piece. "Want one?"

She shook her head no.

"Your brother? Is that where your pain comes from?"

"Some, but I'm no different than anyone else driving a rig. It can get lonely, even with a partner. I like sleeping in my own bed, taking Emma somewhere—"

"Bowling?"

The man was insufferable. Of course he wanted credit for entertaining Emma. She should have seen that coming. He was a pastor, and she needed to remember that.

"Why classical?" She hoped switching the topic of conversation would get his nose out of her business. If they were going to spend every day together, she was going to establish boundaries.

Matthew laughed. It was a man's laugh with a mix of little boy delight. Randi thought she could listen to that laugh forever. She scoffed at herself. Forever? Not likely.

"Why is that funny, Matthew?"

"Because I listen to classical for the same reason. It speaks to my soul, but I like it because I can supply the words. It helps me relax while I'm driving."

"But you've only been driving a big rig for how long?" She checked her speed and set the cruise control.

"I haven't even begun to drive, since you won't let me touch the wheel." Matthew's voice hinted of annoyance.

She fought the feeling of chagrin. "Look, you just finished school. I'm responsible for this load. How do I know you're ready to drive? Besides, the reason you're here isn't to drive, is it? Isn't it to get more converts on the weekends?"

Randi jumped as Matthew slammed his Bible shut.

"That's the idea, and I'm thinking I'm going to start with you."

⁂

A week later, at Greenway Grocers, Randi barked orders at Matthew. "Make sure your mirrors are clean. Are they clean?"

"Of course."

"Can you see the back with both of them? Roll your window down so you can look out."

"I can do this, Randi." Matthew put the truck in reverse.

Randi held her breath as Matthew began to back up to the dock. This was the hardest thing for new drivers to accomplish. She'd seen many fail. "Careful," she muttered. "Careful."

The truck stopped. "Look, if you can't stand the pressure,

why don't you get out and wait for me?"

"Don't think I wouldn't like to, Preacher Boy. But *my* job is to make sure you don't break anything."

He scowled at her and looked as though he might say something. Instead, he shrugged his shoulders then hung his head out the window.

"Come on, mate. I don't got all day," the lumper they'd hired yelled from the dock.

"I guess he's thinking he can unload more trucks today, Matthew, if you'd just back up."

She didn't really care if it took Matthew a few extra minutes. This produce company wouldn't unload for the drivers, but they wouldn't let them take things off the truck, either. You had to hire a lumper. And they knew it. There were always several hanging around the gate waiting to "help out," as they called it. *Help themselves, that is.* Their wages came from her pocket. And Matthew's. That made her mood lift. At least she wouldn't have to come up with all the money.

Crack.

Her head flung back against the seat like a piece of wet spaghetti. He'd done it. Backed the trailer smack into the dock. She'd let her guard down for two seconds, and he'd gunned it right into the cement. Dana would be furious with both of them.

"Hey! What's wrong with you? You got a license to drive that thing?" the lumper screamed through the window at Matthew. "That's gonna cost you double. I've got kids to think of."

"So think of them and start unloading," Randi hollered back as she leaned across Matthew. "You aren't hurt, so you've got nothing to complain about."

The lumper swore and jumped up on the loading dock. The rumble of the trailer door lifting filled the awkward silence in the cab.

"You don't have to defend me," Matthew said. "I'm capable of handling insults."

His quiet tone surprised her. The truth was, if someone had taken on her battle, she'd be hopping mad.

"Sure, now I know. But can you handle Dana?"

❧

Mrs. Bell handed Randi the letter as soon as she walked in the door. "It's from your brother. I saw him today, and he asked me to give it to you. You need to read it."

"And hi to you, too, Mom." She took the note, noticing it wasn't in an envelope. "Did you read this?"

"No. He only asked me to deliver that to you, not read it. It's between you and him."

She eyed her mom suspiciously. "And he didn't say what was in it?"

Her mother shook her head. "I'm so worn out between worrying about A.J. and watching Emma." She sank onto the upholstered rocker and pulled a lap quilt over her legs. "Does it feel chilly in here? Emma keeps telling me it's too hot."

"It is warm in here." Randi helped herself to a butterscotch candy from a jar on the coffee table before she sat in the chair. She read the note then read it again. "You're sure you don't know what he wants, Mom?"

"What's it say?" Her mother leaned in to listen.

Randi's foot tapped against the hardwood floor as her anger toward her brother built. "He wants me to adopt Emma. You know I can't do that. Did you tell him I would?" The note in her hand shook. "What kind of father gives his kid away?"

"One who's not going to be able to take care of her. He's doing it out of love."

"Fine time for him to think about loving her now. He should have considered that before cooking meth in his garage." She crumpled the letter and shoved it into her jeans pocket. "Too bad her mother didn't stick around."

"Don't call that girl a mother. All she did was birth that kid. Giving up her rights to Emma less than a day after she was born. . ." Her mother sighed.

"And now he wants to do the same. Well, I'm not doing it. I love Emma, but it doesn't feel right to legally say he can't be involved in her life anymore. And why me?" She jostled her leg up and down. "I know what you're thinking, Mom."

"You're the best for her, Randi. I wish you could see that. She loves you and you love her. You'd make a great mother."

"But I didn't make that choice." She hated the rush of adrenaline that made her move when agitated.

"Randi, even when you're married you don't always get to make that choice. Some women don't ever get the opportunity to have children. And here you are, not married, and you have the chance to have a wonderful daughter."

"You aren't playing fair, Mom." She had to leave before her mother entangled her deeper in her brother's web. She vaulted from the chair, ready for flight, as Emma, pink-cheeked from the sun, burst through the front door.

"Aunt Randi! You're back!"

She sucked in her breath as the joy of seeing Emma hit her heart. She looked over at her mother. Yep, just what she'd expected. Her mother's lips were moving. *Praying. Always praying.* "Hey, kid, where've you been?"

"At Samantha's. She's my new friend." Emma's smile brightened. "Are we going to meet Matthew tonight?"

"I have to go to work tomorrow and have to get up early."

"I don't like it when you're gone for days. Grandma says you're a teacher, so how come you drive a truck?" Emma's excitement was snuffed like a burning candle in the wind, and she plopped on the floor.

Because I didn't want to come home to an empty house. She wouldn't admit that, though. Her mother would say there wasn't any reason to work to avoid loneliness, not when Emma could be with her *forever*. So she said the next thing she thought of to distract Emma. "Matthew wants to take us to his farm."

Emma bounced off the floor, smacking into Randi and hugging her tight around her waist. "Cows! I get to play with cows!"

Guilt claimed another room in the chambers of her heart. She'd never counted on someone needing her. And now if she didn't want to disappoint Emma, she would have to ask Matthew if they could come.

"When? When can we go?" Emma's voice reached a note high enough to break a fine piece of crystal, if Randi's mother had owned any.

"Soon. I'll tell him you want to go when I see him."

"Can't we call him, Aunt Randi?" Emma pleaded, still dancing around the room. "Can Grandma go, too?"

"Don't worry about me. I'd rather stay here than traipse around a smelly farm." Randi's mother put the rocker in motion. "It will be good for the two of you to spend time together, though."

Randi scowled. She didn't know if her mother meant Randi and Emma, or Randi and Matthew.

thirteen

"This has to be the best food we've eaten yet." Matthew finished his last bite of garlic mashed potatoes. He wiped his mouth with his napkin and laid it on the table.

"They are good. There's a rumor the cook trained at a cooking school in France, Chez Louie or something. He had a job at a restaurant in New York but didn't like living there, so he came back home to Wyoming. But no one has ever found out if it's true or not." Randi looked at her plate, which was still half full.

"I suppose it doesn't matter where he trained as long as it's good. Guess you're ready to go?" Matthew slid out of the booth before withdrawing his wallet. He flipped it open and put a generous tip in the middle of the table. She'd come to recognize that as a signal he'd spotted a wandering sheep, as he called them.

"I think so. Yes, I'll pay yours," Randi said in answer to his unasked question.

"Thanks." Matthew handed over a ten-dollar bill. "That should be enough. I see someone I want to talk to for just a minute."

"I'll pay, but then I'm leaving." Randi snapped up the ticket from the table and crunched it in her hand. Matthew had been riding with her for only three weeks, and it seemed every time they stopped, he had someone he needed to see. It always took him longer to get to the truck than it did Randi. This time she wouldn't wait for him. It wasn't his turn to drive, anyway. If he wasn't sitting in the seat when she wanted to pull out, well, then he'd better be finding a way to meet her down the road.

81

She started for the checkout counter. Anticipating the heat outside, as she walked she removed the denim shirt she wore into the cold, air-conditioned restaurants.

"Randi!"

She turned at the familiar voice. "Elsie and Margaret! It's been about two months since I've seen you." Randi admired these women drivers. They each had teamed with their husbands until two years ago, when Margaret's husband died from a heart attack. After a drunk driver killed Elsie's husband not long afterward, the women had decided to team up. They chose a vivid pink for their truck and used sparkly gold paint to letter *Groovy Grannies* across the front hood. They hauled when they felt like it and stopped to visit their kids and grandkids often.

"I promised my granddaughter Kristen I would always be there the first day of school," Elsie said.

"But it's not even September yet," Randi said.

"She's on that odd schedule where they rotate the kids through the system, so her first day comes early." Elsie placed her napkin on her lap. "She's such a good kid, and I've managed to keep my promise for six years."

"I bet when she hits high school she won't care if you're there the first day anymore." Margaret laughed. "They get family-independent then."

"Not my Kristen. She's knows what's important. Can you sit down and visit for a moment?"

"Maybe you can help us decide on one of these fancy motor homes. Our kids want us to give up driving a rig." Elsie held up a shiny brochure.

"I'm not getting involved in that decision. You're old enough to know what's best for yourselves." Randi glanced at the picture of the RV. "It's not pink, though; that doesn't seem like one you'd like."

"Exactly what we've been saying." Elsie dropped the

brochure on the tabletop.

"Ladies, it's been nice seeing you, and I'd like to slide in and talk to you, but I've got to get moving as soon as I can get my partner away from his congregation."

"We heard a rumor about you riding with a preacher." Elsie leaned forward, waiting as if she didn't want to miss anything Randi had to say.

"It's true. Jess is still on disability, and I've been assigned to have Preacher Boy tag along with me."

"You have to sit for a minute and tell us how Jess is doing. That poor girl. And I can't believe they haven't caught the person who did it yet."

Randi sank into a chair between the women. "She's struggling to get the use of her arm back. The physical therapist is making her use heavy weights, and it hurts. She told me they would make good weapons. Sounded like she might even use them like that, or threaten to." Randi smiled. "Jess is a fighter. She'll be okay."

"What about you? You aren't afraid to drive?" Elsie patted Randi's arm. "Such a frightening experience."

"No, I'm fine." Randi thought about the nightmares that woke her several times a week. Afraid her friends' maturity gave them the ability to detect a lie, she went for distraction. "Want to see a new picture of Emma?"

"Just one?" Margaret smiled. "I thought you would have more than that with you."

"If I had known I would see you today, I would have brought more." Randi flipped open her wallet and slid a photo from its plastic cover. Emma had sat behind the wheel of the rig, pretending to be a driver, when Randi snapped the shot. She placed it in Margaret's waiting hand.

"She has your smile." Margaret passed the photo to Elsie.

"Except Randi has front teeth."

"You know what I mean, Els."

"I remember my Lynn at that age. Seems like she was all teeth and ears. It doesn't seem that long ago." Elsie patted her heart. "My memories just don't let those kids grow older."

A lump formed in Randi's throat. What if her mom was right? Could it be that Emma might be the only child in her life to love? She would be if Randi didn't start letting someone like Matthew into her life. *Matthew!* Why did it have to be his name that came to mind? She had no desire to be a pastor's wife.

"I need to get back on the road, ladies." Randi waved a hand at Matthew, catching his attention, then pointed to her watch.

Matthew nodded and kept on talking to the small group of drivers gathered around him.

"Mmm, mmm, he's a good-looker, Randi. Are you thinking he might be a partner for life?" Margaret grinned at Randi. "I've always loved trucker weddings."

"Me, too," Elsie added. "Make sure you let us know when the wedding is, and we'll get there."

"No wedding! You two matchmakers will have to find another party to attend. Jess will be back soon, and Matthew will be on his way." Randi glared at Matthew. "Besides, he's way too preachy for me."

"You've got that love look in your eyes, girl," Elsie said, handing Emma's picture back.

Randi took the photo and stuck it in her back pocket. "Think again. I'll catch up with you later." As she walked to the checkout, Randi could hear the rowdy laughter of the Groovy Grannies. She felt herself flush as she imagined what they were saying about her and Matthew.

She paid the bill then decided she couldn't pass up the black licorice in the candy stand. After digging out change for her purchase and plopping it onto the counter, she gave Matthew one more pointed look and went to the truck.

She checked her watch. Five minutes. That's all she would give Preacher Boy to finish his praying. She did the mandatory pre-check, noting that the fuel level in the reefer tank maintained an acceptable level. She climbed into the sleeper cab and out of habit began to straighten things, even though she hadn't slept in back since Dana had forced her to ride long hauls with Matthew. Matthew had left his guitar on the bunk. She picked it up and started to put it in its case, then decided to practice the few chords he'd taught her. If he wasn't back by the time she finished, then she'd leave.

Her fingers burned from the strings. She'd done it, played through the chords without forgetting where her fingers were supposed to be. Satisfied with her performance, she placed the guitar on the red silk lining and closed the scratched black cover.

Still no Matthew. She opened her licorice and chewed a piece. Like a child, she stuck out her tongue to see if it had turned black. Her eyes crossed. She climbed into the driver's seat and looked into the side mirror. Not only had her tongue turned dark, but her teeth as well. Satisfied it was the real stuff, she finished it.

She checked her mirrors, hoping to see Matthew's reflection. Not there. Fine. She started the engine, put it in gear, and rolled past the front of the truck stop, slowing to a stop. No Matthew.

"That's it. A person can't be expected to wait forever." Infuriated, she let the clutch out, and the truck tires engaged. Not looking back, Randi threw the gearshift forward and rolled off the lot.

❧

Matthew knew Randi would be furious with him for making her wait—again. He had tried to explain to her how he couldn't walk off and leave someone who'd asked him for prayer. Right now he was talking to Tim, who needed counseling because he thought his wife might be having an affair. He needed someone to talk to, so Matthew had found Brad, another Christian driver who had been through this situation himself. He volunteered to help Tim.

Outside at last, Matthew walked to where he had parked. He ran his fingers through his hair and looked around. Where did the truck go? He parked it right here, next to the rig hauling boats, didn't he? He turned in a circle, his hand over his eyebrows to shield his eyes from the sun. His sunglasses were in the truck, and the truck was. . .where? A panicked feeling hit him. She wouldn't have really left him, would she? Randi had probably pulled the truck to the other side of the truck stop to scare him. He'd be in for a lecture, no doubt.

He jogged around the outside of the brick truck stop, expecting to see Randi leaning up against the door, tapping her finger on her watch the minute he appeared.

No truck.

She had left him.

Left him without a ride.

"Hey, good-looking. Need a lift somewhere?"

Turning at the sound of the voice, Matthew found two older women smiling at him.

"I'm Elsie, and this"—she used her key chain to point at the other woman—"is Margaret."

"We're the Groovy Grannies," Margaret chimed in. "Seems like Randi done ran off and left you. We'll give you a lift if you want. We're heading in the same direction."

Offering a quick thank-you to God for getting him a ride, Matthew said, "Terrific. Which rig is yours?"

Margaret and Elsie both pointed to the pinkest truck Matthew had ever seen.

"That's, uh, a pretty bright truck."

"That's the best truck on the road. Come on, or we won't catch up to Randi anytime soon." Margaret slipped her arm through Matthew's. "I have a grandson about your age."

"You can tell him all about the grandkids when we're driving, Margaret. He'll be asking about the gallery, anyway."

Gallery? Matthew wasn't quite sure what to make of these two, but he guessed he wouldn't be bored.

Inside the truck, when Matthew climbed through the middle to sit in the sleep cab, he realized what the women meant by the gallery. He couldn't miss it. Every conceivable flat space had a picture attached to it. All of children, and not all studio shots. Most were candid, caught when the subject least expected to be photographed.

"How many grandchildren do you two have?"

"Between the two of us, fourteen," Elsie said.

"Fifteen any day now, remember?" Margaret said with pride.

"I could never forget, dear Marge. You tell me at least three times a day."

"She's aggravated with me; that's why she called me Marge. She knows I don't like that name."

"What did your momma name you? I'm sure it wasn't Preacher Boy," Elsie asked as she pulled onto the highway.

"Matthew Carter. Preacher Boy is my handle."

"And why is that?" Margaret asked. She retrieved a basket of red yarn from the floor, set it on her lap, and began knitting something with tiny needles.

"Well, that's obvious, Margaret. The boy is a pastor."

"And why is that obvious? He doesn't have a sign on his shirt, Elsie."

"Weren't you listening when Randi said he was holding church services?"

"It's about time somebody did something like that. Especially now that we have so many women drivers. Maybe it will cut down on the likes of those like Liz Martin. I wonder what happened to her." Margaret's needles clicked in time to her words.

Matthew sat back and watched the women, thinking he wished he and Randi could talk with the ease of these two.

"Liz. Oh, that girl. Keeping two jobs at once, driving a rig, and sleeping anywhere but her own sleeper," Elsie said.

"I bet she saw the ceiling of every cab from here to California." Margaret shook her head. "Such a pretty girl, too."

"Maybe we shouldn't gossip with Matthew in the back, Margaret."

Matthew was startled to be brought back into the conversation. He'd thought they might have forgotten about him. "Gossip is never a good thing. It seems to come back and hurt more people than you think."

"He's right, of course."

Elsie nodded in agreement with Margaret.

Tired from driving most of the morning, Matthew closed his eyes and leaned against the padded cab wall. In his repose he said a silent prayer for Liz.

A few minutes of silence passed. Matthew was almost asleep when the grandmas began another volley of conversation. He started to open his eyes, but then he heard Randi's name and his. Maybe he would learn something about Randi from their conversation. No, that wasn't right. Eavesdropping would get him in trouble later. Maybe if he asked the right questions, he'd get answers. After all, he wouldn't be gossiping, just trying to find a way to help Randi. At least that's what he told himself.

"Have you known Randi for a long time?" Matthew felt bad about encouraging the two women, but quickly pushed the feeling aside. After all, how could he help Randi if he had so little information about her? After weeks of driving together, he still knew very little about her personal life. She didn't seem to want to share any information about herself. She wouldn't even tell him why she used the name Davis instead of Bell, just gave him a kidlike smirk as if to say, "Wouldn't you like to know?"

"We've known Randi awhile now. Met her like you meet most truckers, at a truck stop."

That wasn't much help. "How long have you ladies been partners?" he asked.

Margaret turned sideways in her seat to face Matthew. "I started riding with my husband. Our last child had flown the coop, and I was bored at home alone all the time. All the other women had husbands to do things with. I hated tagging along to the movies or church functions, so I decided to ride with Mac and learn how to take my turn behind the wheel."

"That's why I started driving, too," said Elsie. "I was plumb fed up with the women in my town. They acted like I would steal their husbands if I was left alone with them too long. Then when I'd mention Arnie was driving to New York with a load of potatoes, I'd get this smirky expression looking back at me. As if I didn't know they were thinking, *Poor woman, her husband's off playing with those nasty women that hang around truck stops.* Then they'd pull the arm of their husband and say something cute like, 'I'm so glad you don't leave me alone the way Arnie leaves Elsie.' No, sir, I don't miss those biddies one bit. I do miss Arnie. He was a great husband. Margaret and I teamed up after they were gone." Her earnest expression reflected back to Matthew in the rearview mirror. "You ought to marry that girl and become a team."

"Marry Randi?" Matthew shook his head and laughed at the unexpected segue. "I always thought married couples should know each other well before they stood in front of a preacher, and I don't know much about Randi."

"What do you want to know? I've always favored putting two people together when they are in such obvious need of one another."

Matthew didn't think he would agree that Randi or he was in any such need. But if it would help him with Randi, who was he to stop the women? He could use the information to lead Randi back to the good and glorious Shepherd. Then again, if it turned out that Randi might have a few feelings toward him, he might not object after all. She did have the ability to steal his breath away with just a look.

"She had a fiancé once. I've never asked her about him, though." Margaret rolled the loose yarn onto the ball, tucked her needles into it, and shoved it onto the floorboard. "I just know it ended ugly."

Matthew wasn't sure how he felt about this news. It might explain why Randi didn't want anything to do with men, but what did it mean for him? Could he win her trust?

"I heard she caught him in bed with their Realtor in the house they were going to buy," Elsie said.

"Why don't you ask her about him?" Margaret said.

Stunned, Matthew couldn't answer her. No wonder Randi carried so much anger at God. *She truly is a tender bird in need of care,* he thought. But could Matthew give her the right kind of care? He didn't know. He would like to think he could with his pastoral training, but there was that attraction he felt for her. He couldn't deny the pull he felt when she smiled at him. Yet he knew better than to date with the intention of saving someone.

"No, I don't imagine that would be a good idea. The woman won't even tell me what her favorite color is. I'm thinking she'd be less likely to tell me about a past fiancé," Matthew said.

"Her favorite color? That's easy. She loves yellow. We were having a conversation one day on the radio about truck colors. Remember, Elsie?"

"That's right. She wanted to know why we picked pink for our truck."

"Bet you're wondering that, too, aren't you, Matthew?" Margaret wore a pleased expression. Matthew knew this was one of those times they'd stressed at the seminary, and he needed to express a great deal of interest.

"It is bright pink," he said with a wry smile. "Unusually bright."

"We picked it because we'd been arguing for days about the color. I wanted navy blue, and Elsie wanted green."

"We were driving east when the sun was coming up," Elsie added.

"And the sky turned the most spectacular shade of pink."

"We both said at the same time, 'That's beautiful.' Then we thought, *Why not? We're girls, so it would be appropriate*," Elsie said.

"And since it would be our first truck together," said Margaret, "kind of like having a baby, you send out announcements. It's just that we drive ours instead of sending them through the mail."

"I get it. Why does Randi like yellow?" Matthew tried to direct the subject back to the most secretive woman he'd ever been around.

"She likes yellow because of the sun. Randi hates cold weather and gray days," Margaret said.

"That's right. Yellow is like a warm summer day, when she can take her shoes off and run in the grass. I think that's how she said it." Elsie checked her side mirror before changing lanes.

"I can see her playing in the yard, barefoot, chasing Emma." Matthew smiled. "She would be a good wife and mom." *Wife?* He must be losing a few brain cells. These two lovely matchmakers had him thinking in a direction he hadn't even considered.

"Look at him, Elsie. He's starting to think family thoughts."

"Maybe we'll be having a trucker wedding in the near future. We should start thinking about the shower," Elsie said.

"Wait a minute, ladies. Who said anything about a wedding?

Don't you two go spreading rumors."

The radio interrupted the conversation. "This is Choco-Chip. I'm looking for a package I left back at Dean's Truck Stop. Did anyone happen to pick it up?" Randi's voice sounded sad to Matthew, or maybe he was just hoping she missed him.

"We've got the Preacher Boy with us, Chip. Where do you want him delivered?" Margaret answered.

"There's a friendly hamburger joint in Kelly Cove that has a big parking lot. Can we meet up there?"

"Will do."

"Out, then."

"Sounds like she's forgiven you for not being in the truck on time." Elsie smiled in the mirror at Matthew.

"Maybe. Or she doesn't want to tell Dana I'm not with her."

fourteen

Randi replaced the mic in its black plastic holder. She was glad Matthew had found a ride with the Groovy Grannies. Relief flooded through her as she realized he might have ridden with Notorious Liz, known for stripping a man with her eyes the instant she met him. Liz wouldn't be good company for a man like Matthew, and not just because he worked for God. She didn't want him in Liz's company. Yet wasn't she just the kind of person Matthew wanted to bring God's Word to?

The seat next to her seemed emptier than ever. She didn't miss *him*, did she? Randi didn't think that could be possible. No, she felt only calmness now that he wasn't in the truck. But she did miss the warm, rich scent of masculinity, the soft strumming of his guitar. His fragrance lingered, and she inhaled the woody scent. She hated to admit it, even to herself, but maybe she was beginning to like having this man around.

She tugged a snapshot of Emma from the visor in front of her. She missed her quirky sense of humor. Maybe she should keep her and let Mom live the life she wanted. Sighing, she put the picture back. Emma's crooked smile touched her heart. Maybe she didn't want to drive a truck forever. She'd been foolish to let one man destroy more than her dream wedding. She'd let Brent have power over the rest of her life, and he wasn't even around.

The sign for Burgers and Beyond stood high above the exit ramp as it flashed orange and red, bright even in the dusky light. Randi pulled off the interstate and maneuvered her rig into the establishment's side parking lot, built for truckers and RVs. The security lights flickered to life. One after the other reflected off a few battered farm pickup trucks.

Not quite sure how long it would be until the Groovy Grannies dropped him by the roadside, Randi decided to wait inside for Matthew. She retrieved the shirt she had thrown onto the floorboard earlier. No need to freeze while waiting for him. She picked up her log book as well. She wanted to record this rest, even if it would be small.

She'd worked double shifts the last three weeks. As soon as she and Matthew finished each day, she headed home and changed into the cream and navy Speedy Delivery uniform. With a peanut butter and jelly sandwich in hand, she'd race out the door and wouldn't return until almost midnight. It was a crazy schedule, but the money bought Emma new clothes.

Emma had come home from school upset. Girls taunted her, calling her "witch" because of the color of her eyes. Not content to bedevil her with just that, they continued with her secondhand clothes and nicknamed her "orphan witch."

Randi couldn't change Emma's eyes and her damaged feelings, but she could help her dress like the others. She understood only too well what Emma felt like, and she intended to do what she could to build Emma's self-esteem. Even if it meant driving when she shouldn't.

As soon as Jess returned to work, Randi could say good-bye to Speedy Delivery, but until then she didn't have a choice. The compensation pay Round the Clock gave her didn't cover what she'd made before on long hauls, and when Dana had pushed, Randi had reluctantly agreed to do two-day runs with Matthew. She and Jess were often paid a bonus when they delivered on time.

Inside the tiny pale green restroom, Randi set her log book on the flat top of the trash can cover. Then she draped her denim shirt over the top.

She grasped the hot water spigot. It spun without friction in her hand, and not a drop trickled from the tap. She twisted the other handle, and the cold water gushed from the faucet. Not caring, she cupped her hands under the frigid stream and splashed the stinging water on her face. Her skin reacted to the cold, flushing and turning bright red as an army of blood cells rushed to warm her. She splashed her face once more then turned off the water.

Whisking a brown paper towel that felt more like cardboard from its stainless dispenser, Randi patted the water droplets on her face and the few that had rained onto her T-shirt. Wadding up the towel, she was surprised by the sudden desire for a soft terry-cloth towel and a tub full of bubbles to soak in. Finishing the fantasy, she added to the mirror, "And the best part, to crawl into a real bed and pull the comforter up under my chin."

Not feeling any more alert, she pushed the restroom door open and headed for the counter for a large coffee with cream. Feeling a bit guilty about leaving Matthew behind, she decided to buy him one as well.

Carrying the steaming Styrofoam cups through the door became a challenge as a small team of girl soccer players came barreling inside. She smiled at the comments flying past her. It seemed they had won their game. Someday, maybe. . .no, better not to go there; she'd been morose enough today. *What is wrong with me?*

Randi looked across the parking lot as a horn bellowed. Sighing with relief, she watched as the pink truck settled to a stop next to hers.

Elsie rolled down her window. "How's the coffee here?"

"I haven't tried it yet. It's too hot. Would you like me to get you some?"

"No, we're okay for now," Elsie said.

"Is Matthew ready this time?" Randi could feel the lack of emotion in her voice. She would admit it only to herself, but she was glad Matthew was back and could drive. She needed to rest.

"He's here. We would like to keep him. He's good company."

"Elsie, you only want to keep him because he has a set of fresh ears to listen to your grandkid stories." Randi smiled, too tired to laugh. "Did you manage to get through all of them?"

Margaret yelled through the open window. "We didn't get near enough time to talk about those babies, Randi. Please. Can we keep him until the next stop?"

Randi felt her chest tighten. She needed Matthew right now. What if he chose not to ride with her tonight? "Margaret—"

Laughter spilled from the truck. Embarrassed, Randi kicked at a French fry someone had dropped on the ground.

Matthew walked around the front of the truck. "I'm here, Randi. I'd love to ride with those ladies some more, but I don't think I would get a chance to drive. They like it too much. Did you know they fight over who's driving next?"

Randi felt her mood lighten. For some reason she wanted to hug him, relieved she wouldn't have to drive. That was the reason she felt so happy, right? It didn't have anything to do with the smile he gave her. Did it? It had to be knowing he would be able to take her place behind the wheel, and nothing to do with the tremors his voice sent rippling through her.

"I bought you coffee." Randi thrust the cup into Matthew's hand. "We need to be going."

Matthew nodded. He walked to Elsie's open window. "Thanks for the lift, ladies."

"You can catch a ride with us anytime, Matthew," Elsie said. The pink truck crept forward. "We'll see you down the road."

Matthew waved as the pink truck rolled out of the parking lot. "I'm glad I had the chance to ride with them for a while. Randi, I've been thinking. Is it possible for me to ride along with different drivers sometimes? I think it would be a good way to get to know them."

"No. Not with me, anyway. After Jess comes back, you can try setting up that arrangement with the next person you drive with." Fuming to herself, Randi opened the truck door, stepped up, and settled herself behind the steering wheel. He didn't even apologize for making her stop to pick him up, or even for making her track him down. Never mind that exhaustion ruled her body. She'd drive her own truck. He could sit counting the stars for all she cared.

Randi slammed the door. If he planned to come with her, he had better be running around the truck and planting his behind in that seat right now. Ride with someone else? Why should that bother her? The scary thing was, it did. She shook off the feeling, deciding it must be from lack of sleep. She wrapped her seat belt around her. Wasting no time, she turned the ignition key.

Matthew opened the door, and the dome light flooded the cab. "Randi, I need to apologize for not being ready when you were. I'll try to be on time from now on. It's just that when someone is hurting, I find it's awful hard to walk away from them."

Whipping her head around to face Matthew, Randi said through clenched teeth, "Yeah, well, Mr. Preacher Boy, because of you, my back is hurting from the tension of wondering if I had to go back and get you. It didn't let up just because I found you with the grannies."

"Then let me drive, Randi. Please. There isn't any reason for you to be sitting there now. You could climb in the back, pull the covers over you, and sleep until we get to the motel in Casper." Matthew placed his hand on her shoulder.

The gentleness of his touch and the tenderness in his eyes did it. Tears began to well, threatening to spill over. Trying to hide her reaction to his concern, she unbuckled and jumped out of her seat. "Fine, it's yours. Don't wake me until we get there." She hustled to the back of the cab, not waiting for a reply.

fifteen

Pleased with finding a shortcut through Sublet County, Matthew thought about how proud Randi would be when she woke and found they were closer to their delivery point than they planned to be. The company would be pleased the trip had been made without charging a motel room. Then again, there was that rule on the contract he'd signed. Just because he thought it better to drive through the night this time, it didn't mean they would agree. He hoped when he explained that Randi had fallen asleep before they arrived in Casper and he was confident he could drive through the night, letting her sleep. . . Still, it was their rule—but maybe this once they'd be okay with it. They would have saved the price of a motel room. As he drove, Matthew watched brilliant pinks and blues fill the morning sky. He loved this time of day. He felt closest to God just as the sun peeked through with a nudge then surged into radiant light. For years he had tried to catch God painting the same sunrise, but so far, Matthew had not seen the same one twice. The colors were often the same, but never the way they were displayed in the sky. God definitely held the highest art award for creativity.

He glanced over his shoulder to see if Randi stirred yet. After she went in the back last night, he hadn't heard anything from her, not even a rustle of the bedclothes. Funny, she hadn't even bothered to pull the separating curtain between them. Soon the morning rays would hit her face unless he could reach the curtain and slide it.

Matthew stretched, catching the fabric with his fingertips. He drew the curtain and cringed as the metal grommets scratched loudly against the rod.

Satisfied that Randi remained undisturbed, he turned his attention back to the road. Or tried to. The soft sleeping face in the back invaded his thoughts as it had all night. She had kept appearing in his thoughts as he drove through the night. The sun had not managed to dispel her image from his brain. He thought about the dark circles under her eyes and tried to remember if they were there when he first met her. He didn't think so. Maybe Randi was the kind of driver who had to take a few days off to recharge. He didn't know, but he was sure he wouldn't ask her. Their relationship was tenuous now. No need to make it worse.

There were a lot of questions he wanted to ask her. But how? The two grannies had not solved any of the mystery surrounding Randi. Instead, they'd only made him more curious about this beautiful partner he drove with. If only Randi would trust him. Matthew knew she didn't, and he wondered if it was because he was a pastor. He rubbed his forehead with the back of his hand and squinted at the road before him. It was a shame, because this woman had somehow managed to creep past the barriers around his heart and begun to star in his dreams.

"Matthew, it's morning?" Her voice, soft as silk, called to him from the back. "Where are we?"

"Still headed east. I found a shortcut last night and you were sleeping so soundly, I thought I might as well keep driving instead of pulling in at a motel. Are you hungry?" He ran his hand over his stubble-covered chin. He needed a shave.

"Hungry. Did you call in and tell Dana we would be driving all night?" The curtain grommets dragged against the metal bar. Matthew caught a glimpse of a slender bare foot and red toenails as Randi plopped into the seat next to him dressed in yesterday's shorts and T-shirt.

"No. Didn't think I needed to." He tried to keep his eyes ahead, but not before noticing how beautiful she looked in the bright morning light. Her tousled hair begged him to run his hands through it. He stole a quick glance. She sat with her knees drawn to her chest, feet on the seat. She definitely looked like someone he wanted to wake up to every morning. He focused hard on the road, imagining running his hand across her face at dawn's light, placing a kiss on her cheek, and whispering in her ear how much he loved her.

Love her? He grasped the steering wheel tighter. Matthew didn't know where that feeling came from, but as surely as he knew his middle name was Allen, he knew it was true. He released a heavy breath, sagging back into the well-worn seat with a silent groan. He also knew he couldn't let Randi know. It was a good thing Jess would be coming back soon. Maybe with time away from Randi, he could sort out his feelings. He wanted to make sure it was real love. Not some "I want to bring her to the Lord" love. But he wanted that, too, didn't he?

". . .trouble, you know?"

"What? I'm sorry, I drifted off somewhere, I guess. What did you say?"

"We aren't supposed to spend the night together in the truck, remember?"

"Yeah, I know, but since I was up here and you were back there. . ." He jerked his thumb in the direction of the sleeper compartment. "I figured it'd be okay. And I wasn't the least bit tired. I was wrong. I know it. Guess I thought I'd save the company some money and us some time."

"You don't have to explain it to me. You'll have to justify it to Dana. She's the one who'll decide if you keep driving or not."

"I'm not worried about Dana." Matthew watched Randi stretch her arms over her head, her bare feet to the floorboards. She reminded him of a kitten stretching in warm sunshine.

He longed to reach out and caress her soft skin as he took in the silky smoothness of her bare thighs. He started reciting the verse about being unequally yoked; then he followed with the Ten Commandments in his head, the one surefire way he had of controlling his wayward thoughts.

Only they weren't wayward, were they? Not if Randi wasn't married and he wasn't. Was this God's way of telling him he was meant to share his life with Randi? Was there more to her relationship with God than she had let him know? Sometimes hurt dimmed the light within.

"Why, Randi?" He voiced the question without thinking.

"Why what, Carter?" Randi looked puzzled.

Thinking of another question to ask, he blurted out, "I've been wondering all night why your parents gave you a boy's name. And I really want to know why you use Davis instead of Bell."

"I renamed myself. Sort of. Davis is my mom's maiden name and my middle name. I use it when I drive instead of Bell because it lacks a *feminine ring*, which I wanted to avoid on the road." Randi yawned. "In kindergarten I decided Randi was easier to say and spell. You try writing Miranda when you're five years old. Takes way too long. A.J. wouldn't even take the time to say it. He called me Mira, only I thought he was saying "mirror." The kids at school added Bell to that and I became Miracle Mirabelle."

"So as a child you exhibited independence?" Matthew sat straighter, satisfied as a tick on a dog that he'd discovered something more about her. He chuckled at the look on Randi's face. "Hey, I do know a few four-syllable words."

"I'm sure you do. I just hadn't heard you use them. Maybe you save them for your sermons?"

"Why not come Saturday night and hear for yourself?" Matthew hoped he hadn't pushed too hard. "You could keep a tally of how many I use."

"Not going to happen, Matthew." Randi retrieved a bottle of lotion from the door cubby. With a small squeeze, she poured the vanilla scent into her hand then applied it to her legs.

"But I could use you."

She stopped in midrub, her hand motionless on her leg. "Use me? For what? An example of what a Christian isn't?"

"No. I need a guitar player." Matthew flashed his most charming smile, his gaze avoiding the sleek lines of her long, graceful legs.

"I don't know the music."

"You've heard me play a few of the songs. Besides, they're easy, just a few chord changes, the ones you know."

"I don't think so." She resumed smoothing the lotion in long strokes.

"Please. It's much better when I don't have to sing alone. You could bring Emma." Matthew kept his sight trained on the road before him, not daring to look sideways.

"No doubt. You don't sing, Matthew. You howl."

"Miranda, please."

"Ouch, first-name use. You must be desperate." She snapped the lid on the lotion.

"You can learn the music while we drive."

"How many songs?"

"Maybe six?"

"So you sing instead of preaching a sermon?"

"Sometimes I just give out the message in small pieces."

"You mean, like, sneak it in there?"

"I suppose some might think of it as sneaking." He eyed her with a faint smile. "I think of it as important things needing to stand on their own merit."

Matthew waited for her response, hoping she was seriously considering learning the songs. She seemed to be deep in thought. Should he say anything? Could he say anything to encourage her to participate in a service she said she didn't believe in? If she did agree to play the guitar, could he hold out the hope that Randi wasn't as averse to God as she let on? And if that were true, could there be a chance for a relationship together? He tried to control his excited heartbeat. He said a silent prayer. *Please, God, if Randi is the wife You want for me, give me a sign, and I'll charge on full throttle. If not, please stop making her smell so good.*

sixteen

Randi ran her tongue over her teeth. They felt fuzzy. She hated this part of OTR driving—morning breath—waiting until a rest stop to brush your teeth and comb your hair. Pulling her fingers through her hair, she tried at least to get it to lie in the right direction. She should have braided it before going to sleep, but she'd been too tired. She would pay for that when she endured the pain of dragging a comb through the long, tangled mess.

Glancing at Matthew, she wondered what he was thinking about. He seemed stressed. Probably because she hadn't agreed to play the guitar for him. She should. It couldn't be that hard to learn the music. It seemed to her that he played the same three chords. But would he expect her to do it more than one time? That she couldn't do. But it might be interesting to hear him give a sermon. Not that she bought into that stuff anymore, not since she'd learned the only person she could count on was Randi Davis. But maybe she could think of it as live participatory theater.

She stole a wary glance at Matthew and exhaled loudly. "I'll do it, Matthew. Just this once. This time and, I repeat, this time only." Had she really said that? She needed a strong cup of coffee before she found herself agreeing to anything else.

"Okay!" Matthew beamed.

She couldn't believe it, but Preacher Boy glowed. Unreal. If agreeing to play guitar for him gave him that look, what would happen if she reached over and planted a kiss on that gorgeous face? Randi mentally slammed herself back into the seat. She had lost her mind. Gone for sure was any common sense. Jess had to come back, and fast. If she didn't, Randi would be a pulpy mess.

"Looks like flashing lights ahead."

"Portable scales ahead: Trucks use right lane." Randi read the sign along the shoulder and groaned. "I hate ugly surprises so early in the morning. Matthew, we have to get weighed and inspected before we can get our first cup of coffee."

"Looks that way. A good stretch won't hurt me any. Can you hand me my log book, please? They're going to ask for it." Matthew pointed to the floorboard at her feet. "I tossed it down there. Might as well hand me yours, too."

Randi reached into the side pocket in the door. Her breath rate increased and her hand shook as she pulled it back, empty. "Matthew." She hated how her voice sounded small, smaller than the mewling of a newborn kitten. "I don't have mine."

"Why not?"

"I remember setting it on the trash can at the hamburger place with my shirt. I'm sure I left it there."

He glanced over at her, his eyebrows furrowed. "You have the duplicates, right? So there won't be a problem."

She squeezed her eyes tight, afraid to tell him.

"Randi?" His voice held a hint of panic.

"I don't have them. I don't like loose papers, so I don't tear them out of the book."

Matthew's fingers tightened on the wheel; his knuckles were white. "Maybe they won't ask to see it this time."

"They'll ask, and I'll be out of service for at least twelve hours." Randi examined the chipping paint on her fingernail and wished she weren't here. Jess would laugh this off, but Matthew didn't look like he found anything humorous about the situation.

"And I can't drive much longer because I've almost been behind the wheel for ten hours. That means I won't make my Saturday night service." The gruffness in his voice filled the cab.

"Matthew, I'm sorry. I've never done this before." Randi looked at him. His jaw sharpened, and his cheek was thumping. She couldn't blame him for being angry with her. If he had left his log book, she would be screaming in his face right now, not sitting there quietly biting back words.

"It's okay if you yell at me, Matthew." She leaned back against the seat and waited for an inferno of anger.

"No, Randi. Everyone makes mistakes. It will mean calling people, but I'll just have the service during the week." He slouched back into the seat.

Randi wished he would yell, smack the steering wheel with his hand, or something. She hunkered down in her seat. His quiet acceptance—the forgiveness routine—just made her feel worse.

&

In the side view mirror, Matthew could see a line of trucks stretching far behind them. They had moved to the front, one tire length at a time. A Wyoming Department of Transportation officer stood at the back of the scales. If they were the correct weight, he would signal.

Matthew was relieved when they were waved forward. Just past the scale, another officer held up his hand for them to stop.

He stepped over to Matthew's open window. "I need to see your log books."

Ready for him, Matthew gave it to him. "Here's mine."

"She a driver?" He pointed at Randi. "I'll need hers, too."

"Yes, but she left her log book at the restaurant in Kelly Cove. She's been resting for ten hours. I wouldn't lie to you. I'm a pastor."

The officer raised the sunglasses from his nose and peered at Matthew. "Then you should know what rules are all about. You may be a pastor, you might be a guy with a dot-com divinity degree, and it don't matter to me. No book, no driving. Pull your truck over to the side."

Matthew clamped back a reply. No point in making the man angry. Besides, he still had a chance to talk to the guy while he inspected the truck.

"This isn't good. He's going to find something wrong with the truck. They always do." Randi's posture was so straight Matthew thought a strong wind wouldn't budge her.

"Don't be a pessimist. I'll talk to him. Maybe he'll change his mind." He pulled the door handle.

"And maybe pigs do fly."

He ignored her and climbed out of the truck.

The WDOT officer circled the truck with a clipboard in his hand. He took the pen from behind his ear and wrote something down. Matthew leaned over, trying to read the writing.

"Back off, son."

Matthew heard the truck door close. Randi came around the back of the trailer. He waved her away. This guy was irritated about something, and the look on Randi's face didn't indicate someone who cared. She glared at him then turned back.

"Is something wrong, sir?" Matthew put his hand in his jeans pocket and rubbed the tiny cross he kept there to remind him that Jesus didn't die just for him, but even for WDOT officers.

The officer raised an eyebrow. "That's what I'm looking for. Why don't you wait over there?"

"Sure." Matthew glanced back to make sure Randi wasn't lying in wait for the guy, then headed for the office. Unease filled his mind. He had broken the rule of driving together at

side. Thoughts like these were not the kind one should be thinking about a man who preached God's Word. She had to distance him from her thoughts, banish the feel of his heartbeat from her soul. And forget the way he smelled.

"You're going to need a new log book. And you said you were hungry, so do you still want to stop at the truck stop? Or can I keep driving until we reach the town where we'll be staying?" Matthew's rich voice broke into her thoughts.

"Keep going. We'll pick up a new log at the next truck stop. I can tear a page out of yours to use until I get one. Besides, I'm not hungry anymore." *At least not for food,* she thought. *I wonder what those lips would feel like on mine.*

Shocked at her desire, Randi realized she had it bad for this preacher man. How had she let this happen? It had to be Dana's fault for pairing them together. *Maybe that's the problem. We've been spending too much time together, so naturally I would begin to find him attractive. Wonderful.* Now she was admitting even more to herself. More than she wanted to.

"I'm hungry, but I can wait. It won't take long to get there." Matthew rubbed her shoulder.

"I'd better tell Dana we're stopping for that mini vacation." Randi reached for the mic and tried to pretend she didn't enjoy the warmth left by his hand. "This won't be pleasant."

"I guess they get mad when something like this happens."

"It's not just the dispatcher; it's everyone who's listening when you call it in. Every truck stop we pull into, drivers will be snickering beneath their baseball caps."

"Only because they're glad it didn't happen to them. If you're worried about that, why don't you use your cell phone?"

"It wouldn't make any difference. The word will get out even faster if they think I'm trying to hide it." Randi took a deep breath and called the dispatcher.

seventeen

The back-up signal beeped as Matthew backed the truck into the only spot large enough in the rear lot of the Sleep-Inn. Behind him loomed a privacy fence.

"Don't hit it."

"Just because I hit a loading dock once doesn't mean I'll crash that fence." He didn't know if he was trying to reassure himself or Randi.

"We'll just make sure." She opened her door and hopped out.

He could see her in the mirror as she motioned him back. *Two cents and I'd ram into it, just to watch her face.* His face frowned back at him in the mirror. *Sorry, God—she frustrates me. She can lose her log book and I don't get mad, but this taunting about my driving skills is brutal. You have to help me out here.* He eased into the space and let out a sigh of relief.

Randi met him at the door. "Nice job, Preacher Boy."

He felt his eyebrow rise. She'd given him a compliment? That had to be God working. "Thanks."

Inside the small motel Matthew followed Randi to the reservation desk. He rested his elbows on the counter.

"Can I help you?" The red-haired woman behind the desk tossed a copy of *Soap Opera Review* on the counter.

"We need two rooms for the night," Randi said.

"Can't help you, then. Only got one." The woman retrieved her magazine and settled back in her chair. "You won't find anything else in town, either, not with the Bluegrass Festival going on. Everybody's booked. I only have this room because someone canceled about an hour ago."

"We'll take it," Matthew said.

112

He pulled his wallet out of his back pocket. Flipping it open, he grasped his credit card and slid it onto the counter.

"I need you to fill out this information before I give you the key." She pulled a form out from under the counter and slapped it down in front of him, swiping his credit card in the process.

Matthew scratched the pen across the paper to get the ink flowing.

"There's a queen-sized bed, you know," the clerk said with hesitation while waiting for Matthew's credit to be approved.

"No problem—we're truck drivers." Matthew looked up in time to see the pursed lips of the clerk.

"Well, that makes it okay then, I suppose." She handed him back his card. "We don't have automated checkout here like the big hotels, so you'll have to come back by the front desk before you leave." She took the signed slip from Matthew and passed him the room key.

As soon as the elevator doors closed, Randi broke into laughter.

"What's so funny?"

"You know what she's thinking, don't you? One bed, and it's okay because we're truck drivers?"

Matthew could see where the woman might have misunderstood. His face flushed. "Should I go back and explain that I'll be sleeping in the truck?"

"You're blushing!" Randi hooted. "Don't go. I'm sure by now she thinks I'm a lot lizard. It wouldn't be the first time someone has thought that." Randi sighed and punched 2 for the second floor.

"Who thought you were a prostitute? Why did they think that?" That anyone could think that about Randi made his blood froth with anger.

"I had to take some forced rest time, so I took a book with me to a table at a truck stop to read."

"The universal signal." Matthew shook his head in disbelief.

"I should have known better. A trucker who didn't know me came over and wanted me to check out his sleeping arrangements. I told him I was a driver, not a lot lizard."

"Then he left you alone?"

"No. He kept insisting and even tried pulling me off the chair."

Matthew fell silent. If he'd been there, he would have protected her. A woman should have the right to read a book in public. Her story reinforced his commitment to bring God's love and grace to these people.

The elevator stopped on their floor. A bell dinged as the doors slid open, exposing carpet featuring bright blue, yellow, and orange color bursts. Randi started down the hall in the direction the arrow on the wall pointed.

"So what happened?"

She looked over her shoulder with a smile. "I was about to slug him with my book, but the Groovy Grannies saw what was going on and were all over him like grease on a fire."

"I'm glad they looked after you."

"That was the first time I met them. At first they thought I was a lot lizard, too, but when they saw me struggling with him, they realized I needed help."

Matthew laughed. "So did they hit him or lecture him?"

"Lectured. Turns out they knew him. He had a wife and kids."

"That's a real problem for some drivers, isn't it?"

"For some, but not all. Most of the married drivers wouldn't even consider cheating on their wives. It's a bad-boy image stereotype that's survived from long ago."

Stopping in front of room 215, Matthew slid his card key into the slot and watched for the green light to flash. Quickly he pushed down on the handle and flung open the heavy door. He held it wide and waited for Randi to enter.

He followed her into the tight hallway, past the bathroom door. The queen-sized bed covered with a soft cream-colored spread engulfed the room. The TV sat encased in an armoire. "Be nice to catch a baseball game."

"Typical behavior of the male species." Randi pulled open the heavy dark green curtains. "What a view, if you don't mind looking at concrete and gas station signs."

Matthew turned on the television and began surfing the channels.

Randi yawned and stretched her arms over her head for a moment. "I think I want to take a quick shower to wake up and then get something to eat. That means you're out of here."

Out of here? Matthew's attention came back to Randi in a flash.

"How about you?" she asked.

"I'm for grabbing a snack then sleeping. I'll eat later." Matthew looked longingly at the bed. "Sure would be nicer than sleeping in the truck."

"And you're a man of God?" She grinned.

"It would be nice to have room to roll over. I'm tired and want to sleep in a real bed, not something that's stuck in puberty pretending to be king-sized. Why don't you let me have the room?"

"Not a chance, Preacher Boy. You'll be okay out there, I'm sure." Randi batted her eyes at him. "But since I'm the reason we're here, you can use the shower first if you want."

"Nope, you go. I'll wait in the truck."

"I'll be fast, and while you take your shower I can explore the town."

"Thanks. Why don't you find out what this festival is all about and if it's something we want to do tonight? Or at least locate the movie theater. Unless you don't want to hang around with me."

"Who else is there to hang around with, Carter?" Randi

plopped her knapsack on the bed and pulled it open. She pulled out a blue T-shirt and a pair of jeans. "I hope it isn't a dress-up affair. I didn't bring my best clothes along on this trip."

"Not likely. It's a street festival." Matthew processed her last statement. "You have dress-up clothes?"

Randi threw her jeans at him. "Shut up, Carter. I do have a life besides driving a truck."

"What do you do? I haven't heard anything about a man in your life who takes you to the nice places you deserve to go."

"I make myself happy. I don't need a man to go to nice places, thank you very much. Jess and I go to the theater in New York and stay the weekend."

"The theater in New York?" Matthew found this to be another interesting facet of Randi. How many more barriers lay locked under that protective layer she wore? And how long would it take him to get the right key?

"Sure. We've been to a few Broadway shows. My favorite place to stay is the Broadway Inn. It's like a bed-and-breakfast, only not in the country. Once you leave the inn, everywhere you turn there's something fun to do—Times Square, the Manhattan Mall."

"Do you get all dressed up, too?" Matthew scratched his head. This just didn't seem like the Randi he thought he knew.

"Of course we get dressed up for shows. It wouldn't be any fun if we didn't. Slinky dresses and stiletto heels make you feel fabulous."

"Stiletto heels?" Matthew tried to stop the rapidly forming picture of Randi's graceful legs rising from those shoes.

"I'm kidding, Carter. About the heels, anyway. I can't walk in anything that high."

Matthew sighed in relief as the image of her legs popped and replaced itself with the Randi he knew, wearing tennis shoes, faded jeans, and a three-sizes-too-big denim shirt.

"I'm hitting the shower. I'll come by the truck when I'm done and give you the key before I go exploring." She took the remote from his hand.

"Guess that's a polite way of saying I need to leave." He held up his hand to silence the words forming on her lips. "I'm out of here. Enjoy the shower." He hustled out the door, desperately trying to brush away the image of a world where Randi wore high heels and a dress with slit sides. When that didn't work, he added a white apron and a pan of lasagna. He grinned, knowing he would only see that in his dreams.

eighteen

Refreshed from her shower, Randi felt ready to take on the town. The motel desk clerk had told her the business district was within walking distance. She intended to explore and see what it had to offer. She opened the truck door, held on to the chrome side rail, and pulled herself inside. "Matthew?"

No reply other than the sound of deep breathing. She peeked into the sleeper cab. Matthew was sprawled on the bed asleep. She hovered over him for a moment, stilling the hand that wanted to stroke his cheek. Something about his sleeping face comforted the ache within her. She couldn't understand why he should be the one to comfort her, but he did. He seemed so full of peace. She wished she could sleep that way, with the serenity Matthew had, but longing for it wouldn't change anything.

She hesitated for a moment longer then reached over and touched his shoulder. "Shower's free."

He grumbled something unintelligible.

She poked him in the side with the motel key card. "I'm leaving the key on the seat."

He mumbled something that sounded vaguely like "thanks" then rolled over with his arm stretched across his face.

Randi gave him one more look and decided not to try to wake him any more. He needed to rest. She slipped out the door and eased it shut.

She headed for the street the clerk had told her would have clothing shops and a place to get something to eat. *Interesting little town,* she thought as she turned the corner. Jess would have loved exploring it with her. At the entrance to the street stood two brick columns to block cars from entering. An iron arbor connected the two with WELCOME spelled out on the top. The street paved with cobblestones beckoned her to walk and shop.

Sweet pastry smells wafted from a bakery. She could see the sign hanging from a striped awning. Its quaint chalkboard sign boasted of freshly made apple cinnamon muffins. Adding one of those to a steaming cup of coffee or tea would be perfect before starting her search for something suitable to wear for the evening.

Muffins and cakes piled high on glass stands inside the bakery made it difficult to stick with her first choice. She hovered in front of a chocolate chip raspberry cheesecake.

"They all look so good," she said to the man behind the counter. Behind her, a bell on the door announced another customer.

"Don't ask me what my favorite is. I change my mind every day," said the man.

The smell of rich dark coffee permeated the air as she chose the special of the day. She ordered a muffin and took her breakfast to eat at the only outside table.

"Do you mind if we join you?"

Randi looked up to see a young woman with a baby on her hip standing behind a stroller. "Sure. I'm Randi."

"I'm Pat, and this," she said as she tapped the baby on the leg, "is Evan. Scott, the bakery's owner, should buy another table for out here. He gets enough business in the mornings. Thanks for sharing with us."

"I don't mind. I like meeting new people. You know the owner?"

"In a small town everyone knows everyone else and what they're doing, it seems. You, for instance, would be the talk of the town if the festival wasn't going on. Lucky for you, you're not the only stranger in town."

"Small towns have that reputation, don't they?" Randi said.

"In this case it's true." Pat smiled.

"How old is Evan?" Randi pulled her tray closer to allow Pat room to set her food on the small table.

Pat sat and balanced Evan on her lap. "He's fourteen months and a handful." She brushed her hand across his tawny hair. "But we love him. Are you here for the festival?"

"No, I'm a truck driver, stranded until tomorrow."

"That's rotten luck. What happened?"

"I left my log book at the Burgers and Beyond in Kelly Cove." Noticing the confused look on Pat's face, she added, "You have to write down the time you drive, and if you get caught without the book, they ground you."

"So you drive alone?"

"No, but my partner had driven almost all the hours he's allowed, so here we are in your little town."

"I suppose you noticed the signs posted everywhere for tonight's festival. You should go. It's quite a big deal around here, and it's surprisingly fun. For a small town, we do a good job. Maybe that will brighten your stay. The food is always good, and they have a band every year."

"I thought I would go, but I need to get something to wear. All I have with me are jeans," Randi said.

"Jeans are fine, unless there's someone you want to dress up for?" Pat laughed. "I'm sorry. That isn't any of my business. I'm just curious and often ask questions before I think."

"I'm with my temporary partner, Matthew." Randi paused; how much did she want to tell this woman, anyway? She missed Jess. She needed another woman to talk to about the feelings she had for Matthew. Besides, Jess would know exactly what Randi should wear.

"Nice name. Is he gorgeous?" Pat took a sip of her coffee.

"Bite! Bite!" The toddler opened his mouth wide.

Pat broke off a piece of muffin and fed it to him. "Here, sweetie."

"He is, but I'm not interested. Well, maybe a little." Randi surprised herself with her answer. "Where is a good store for something casual but cute?"

"Domm's is great. I have some free time if you want help—you know, another woman's opinion. There I go again. I'm impulsive, or so my Bob says. Of course you might not want us to go. Evan is cute, but shopping with him can be a trial some days."

The disappointment on her face made it impossible for Randi to say no. "We can try, right? If he gets fussy, you can always take him home."

"Great. I've been so lonely. My best friend moved about a month ago, and I just haven't found anyone to spend girl time with." Pat wiped a trace of milk from Evan's face with a napkin.

"I've lost my best friend, too. Not lost, exactly. Jess was hurt and can't drive with me for a while. I miss her, even though I call her. It isn't the same as being with her and doing things."

"Like shopping?"

"Exactly, and talking about movies and good books."

"You are in serious need of girl time." Pat began to gather her belongings. "I don't need any more to eat, and Evan's had enough. Let's get started."

"I'll put the trays back inside." Randi couldn't seem to move fast enough.

"Thanks. I'll get Evan back in his stroller while you do that."

When Randi returned, Pat stood waiting behind the stroller with a smile on her face. "I think I'll get something for tonight as well. Bob and I haven't been out for a while, and his mother said she would watch Evan for us."

"It's nice she's able to help you." Randi thought of her mother and how she'd reluctantly agreed to take Emma.

"She's a gem, my mother-in-law. My mom lives a few

states over, and Bob's mom makes me feel like her daughter. Hey, why don't you meet Bob and me tonight for dinner?"

"Sure. I don't think Matthew will mind, and if he does, he can eat by himself."

"He won't want to if we find just the right dress." Pat grinned. "I think something to show off those long legs, and in red."

"If I do that, I'll have to buy shoes!" Randi moaned, trying to sound sad.

"Shoes! Great! And to think I almost went home to eat instead of asking to share your table."

❧

The shadows of the day fingered their way through the streets. Matthew observed how his and Randi's dusky images touched on the street. He entwined his fingers with Randi's, liking the shadow picture even more. She tried to pull her hand from his. "Leave it, will you? It's just so we don't get separated and spend the evening searching for each other."

"If that's the only reason, then I guess that will be okay." Her fingers snuggled tighter against his.

He kept her close beside him as he wove through the crowd that filled the little town's streets. He found it to be a challenge not to knock a food-laden plate or drink from someone's hand. Laughter and shouts of "Hey, didn't think I'd see you here" rang out, causing Matthew's heart to twang in longing for the town fair he would miss back home.

"Where are we supposed to meet your new friends?" He turned to Randi and leaned in close to hear her answer and inhale the pleasant scent she wore.

"Star Galaxy. It's the old movie theater. It's not too far from here."

Matthew navigated in the direction of Randi's outstretched bare arm.

Vendors called from makeshift carts, enticing all to try

their special sauces. Banners in red and white stripes draped from cart edges. Raffle tickets were being sold for a fat tire bike.

Matthew inhaled the luscious smells of brats, burgers, and brisket. Wooden barrels filled with ice and sodas were in easy reach of the sellers. Kegs of beer were stacked high behind some stalls. The silver barrels dripped with perspiration, sending tiny rivers down the street. He frowned for a moment then whispered a quick prayer that no one would be hurt because of the effects of the alcohol being served this evening.

"There they are!" Randi's excited voice sent ripples through Matthew. This woman knew how to have fun, and he was the fortunate guy tonight. *Beyond fortunate,* he thought. Not everyone would have a beautiful woman by his side. Not one dressed in a yellow and white sundress, giving Matthew a hint of Randi's trim shape and plenty of slender legs to view. He would love to be able to run his hands over what appeared to be silky skin. He gave himself a mental shake and forced himself to return to the introductions at hand.

"Matthew, are you listening?" Randi tweaked his chin with her hand.

"Yes, I am. Nice to meet you, Bob and Pat. See? I heard you." Matthew breathed a sigh of relief that he hadn't blundered the names.

Bob winked at Matthew. "I can see why you might be distracted by these beautiful women."

Matthew laughed. "Thanks for the save. Of course these two blinded me with their outstanding beauty, and I lost track of the conversation."

Pat raised her eyebrows. "I don't know, Randi. Matthew may not be as special as you originally thought."

Matthew glanced at Randi. She was blushing.

"I never said he was special. Well, a special pain maybe."

Her defensive tone of voice didn't quell the happiness he

felt from knowing she thought he was special.

"Anybody hungry?" Bob asked.

"I am. I saw a few things that looked enticing on our way here. Did you have a place in mind?" Matthew asked.

"Why don't you and Randi find something and meet Bob and me back here with your dinner? We'll probably have to eat standing." Pat put her hand in Bob's. "It will be nice to eat with grown-ups for a change."

"I like that idea. It should be easier to please two instead of four individual tastes." Randi tugged on Matthew's sleeve. "Let's find our dinner."

They walked down one side of the cobblestone street, over-whelmed by the choices.

"See anything you want to eat yet?" Matthew stood close to her, trying to ignore the pleasant smell of roses coming from her shoulders. She smelled like a July evening; like someone he would love to stroll across a field with and sit beside on a blanket to watch the sunset.

"It all looks good. I can't decide." Randi's face was flushed with excitement. "What if I get something and then walk just a bit farther and find exactly what I wanted? Can we explore both sides of the street, then choose?"

Matthew could feel his stomach rumble. He didn't want to wait, but he would. He would do anything this woman asked of him. If only he could turn her heart toward God. Then life would be just this side of heaven.

"Let's narrow the choices. Why don't we find the stall with the boldest barbecue sauce?"

"And corn dripping with butter." Randi spun a half turn in front of him. "Matthew, over there. Looks like they have what we're looking for."

They carried their meal to one of the small stone-walled planters that lined the sidewalk. Side by side, they sat on the flat-topped wall and waited for their new friends. Across the street in a corner parking lot, a band began to set up. Earlier, someone had pulled two farm trailers parallel to each other for the bandstand. Several sheets of plywood covered part of the asphalt lot to be used as a dance floor. A teenager set up rows of metal folding chairs with MARS FUNERAL HOME stenciled on the backs.

"What kind of music do you think they play?" Randi asked.

"Opera," Matthew said, holding his face as still as possible. "It's a bluegrass festival."

"But there could be an opera written with bluegrass music, right?" Matthew tried to keep from smiling.

"Sure, a cast of opera singers that travels across the country-side in a bus to belt out songs from the tops of trailers. Maybe it's the band scramble Pat was telling me about. The bands don't get a chance to practice together." Randi looked down the sidewalk. "Here come Pat and Bob." She handed her plate to Matthew. "Hold my dinner, please." She climbed on top the wall. "Over here, Pat." She waved, and the couple joined them.

Pat sat down next to Randi. "So many choices of good food. How did you decide so fast?"

"Matthew's stomach kept growling, and I took pity on him and settled for the next booth with corn."

"Seems to me you placed your order before me. Guess that makes you the hungry one," Matthew teased.

"Or made you the polite one," Bob suggested with a wide grin.

"Bob, you and I are going to be great friends. You've rescued me twice tonight already."

"Matthew thinks the band will be doing a bluegrass opera." Randi laughed. "He has to be wrong."

"Guess we'll have to stick around and see," Matthew said. "People are starting to fill the chairs, so it shouldn't take long to find out which opera singer is onstage. I think it will be a woman."

"I suppose you think all great opera singers are women?"

"No, I just think this one is."

Matthew finished his dinner and drank the last of his soda. He noticed Randi's plate still held most of her sandwich. "Aren't you going to finish that?"

"No. I'm stuffed. You want to finish it?" Randi handed her tray to Matthew. "It's good, just too much."

Matthew took the tray from her. "No, I've had enough, too. I'll toss it in the trash for you, though. Anyone else finished?" He gathered trash from Pat and Bob.

He darted in front of a stroller holding two look-alikes. Girls, he thought. He found a trash can, tossed the remains of their meal, and headed back to Randi. She was talking to the owner of the stroller. He watched as Randi bent down and caressed the cheek of the baby nearest her. That motherly touch jolted him. Matthew felt as if God had grabbed him by the shoulders and said, "What's it going to take for you to realize I picked her out for you?"

"Matthew!"

Randi's voice brought him back. He made his way to her side. "What's wrong?"

Her nose crinkled at him, much like a rabbit's. "Nothing's wrong. I wanted to tell you I asked the mother of the twins what kind of band was playing."

"Smug look on your face. Let me guess. It's not opera."

Randi laughed. "Don't be so disappointed, Matthew. It is the band scramble. So I was right. Admit it."

"Yes, ma'am, you are the current champ of Guess the Band." The first notes of a song floated through the air. "Where did the other two go?"

"Out there." Randi pointed to the dance floor. "They couldn't wait for the music to start. Something about not wasting a minute of their time without the baby."

"Do you dance, Randi?"

"Not a chance."

"Me, either." He sat close enough to her that he could feel her swaying to the music. "But we could walk around and maybe feel the rhythm through the soles of our feet?"

She smiled at him, and he felt like a king.

Matthew held out his hand to her. She hesitated then placed her hand in his. He led her toward the soda vendor. Her fingers entwined with his, and he felt like he held a missing piece of himself. He knew without a doubt he'd given his heart to her.

&.

Bob and Pat finished the dance and joined Matthew and Randi on the folding chairs; Bob handed them both sodas.

"Thanks." Matthew took a drink of the cold refreshment. "I'll get them next."

"No need. We're headed home. Evan should be sleeping. We thought we'd sit on the couch and enjoy some quiet time." Bob took his soda from Pat.

Realizing the end of the evening with her new friends had come, Randi said, "If I ever get to come back this way, Pat, let's meet for lunch or dinner, or. . ."

"Shopping," Pat finished. "I'd like that, too. Try to give me advance notice, and maybe I can get a sitter. Ah, girl time. Just can't get enough of it."

"Great. I'll call you before then, too." Randi hugged Pat.

Matthew shook hands with Bob. "If I'm still driving with Randi, I'll see you as well." He avoided looking at Randi. He didn't have to look at her to know her face would be hard and she'd be quick to deny the suggestion that he would be with her still.

The band started another song with a fast tempo.

"You want to stay?"

"Would you mind if I went back to the motel to sleep? I want to get an early start tomorrow. You can stay."

"No, I'll go back with you."

"But you're not tired yet," she protested, stroking his arm.

"That's okay. Too bad I can't drive again tonight. We could leave now."

"Well, we can't, so let's do what we can now. Before we go, though, let's find a booth selling ice cream for a bedtime snack."

The moon cast a glow on Randi's upturned face. Matthew thought a few kisses from her would be a delicious bedtime snack.

"Randi." He pulled her close to him so that Randi alone would hear the words meant only for her. "You look beautiful tonight."

"Matthew, we'd better get some food into you. You must be light-headed."

"No, I'm fine. That's not why I said you look beautiful."

"Then why would you? Why would you want to ruin a nice evening?"

He frowned down at her. "I'm confused. I tell you that I love the way you look in the moonlight, and you decide the evening is ruined?"

"Moonlight? You didn't say anything about moonlight. What's wrong with you, Carter?" She backed away from him. "I can't let you fall in love with me. Not that I wouldn't like to find out what those brown eyes would look like full of passion, or how your lips would feel against mine, but, Matthew, you're a pastor. It can't—no, it *won't* happen."

"Are you through?"

"For now."

Matthew pulled her close to him and whispered, "Don't say it can't or won't happen, Miranda Davis Bell. If God desires this attraction between us, then it will happen." Before she could protest any further, he brought his lips to hers. At first he could feel her resistance; then his heart soared as she began to kiss him back with an energy that matched his.

The kiss over, Randi pulled away, but her eyes remained locked with his.

A smattering of clapping and a few whistles of approval drew Matthew's attention from Randi. He hadn't meant to make a public display, but he smiled at their approval. Now all he had to do was convince Randi they had a chance at love.

nineteen

Embarrassed by the public display of affection, Randi put her hand against Matthew's chest and gently pushed him back.

"Please don't do that again."

She couldn't allow him to kiss her again. She took a step back and felt resistance from her heart, like a magnet being pulled from its mate.

"I'm going back to the room." She forced the words from her lips.

"Randi, wait. I'm coming with you."

"It's okay, really. I'm a big girl, and I can find my room."

"I'm walking you." His voice held determination.

"Whatever." Determined to remain silent while she sorted out her feelings about the excellent kissing abilities of Matthew Carter, she increased the speed of her steps. The rounded edge of the cobblestone sidewalk jarred her balance, throwing her backward into Matthew's arms.

She felt the pressure of his arms around her, helping her steady herself on her feet. The safety she felt in his arms scared and excited her.

"Thanks, I'm okay now. I'll walk slower."

"I don't mind catching you anytime you fall, Randi."

Matthew's voice soothed her jangled nerves. She gave him a tentative smile of thanks and fell into step next to him. She remained deep in thought, weighing all aspects of a relationship with a pastor.

The motel wasn't far, and they were back at the room before Randi could come to terms with her feelings. Inside, she crossed the room to the drapes. She grabbed the long plastic wand and maneuvered it until the drapes were closed.

"It's not home, but at least you won't have lights shining in your eyes all night." Matthew stood with his back resting on the closed door.

"And no road noise." She turned from the window. The room seemed small with him there. Her hands fluttered, searching for something to do, and she ran them down the front of her dress. "Do you think you'll ever get tired of being on the road, Matthew?" Randi perched on the edge of the bed and slipped out of her shoes.

"I hope not. Right now all I can imagine is driving and preaching for the rest of my life." He sat next to her on the bed. "What about you?"

"I don't know. Sometimes I think I'd like to have the dream." He didn't need to know she wouldn't mind if he starred in it.

He scratched his cheek. "The dream?"

"Yeah. Picket fence, car pool, and orthodontist appointments." *And the urge is getting stronger every day.* Randi visualized herself, Emma, and friends in her car on the way to the mall for a shopping adventure. Everyone smiling and lots of giggles.

"I'm shocked. I would never have guessed you even thought about doing something so normal." He moved to the desk and with one hand spun the chair around until it faced her. He sat across from her.

"Relax. It won't happen. I almost tried it once." She stopped. She'd done it now. He'd want to know the entire story.

"What do you mean?"

Yep, he couldn't help himself. Might as well tell him, Davis.

"I was engaged once. It didn't work out. That's all." *Please don't ask for more.*

Concern washed across his face. "What happened?"

"Not a lot to tell. We were buying a house, and I found Brent in the one we'd chosen, with the real estate agent. Not a stitch of clothes on either one of them. Didn't leave any room for doubt the wedding was canceled."

"He didn't deserve you."

"That's what I said. I decided right then to change my life. I did a one-eighty and quit applying for a teaching job and learned to drive a truck." Randi rubbed a red spot on her foot and winced. "I should have worn my tennis shoes. I think I have the beginnings of a blister."

"And ruined the effect of that dress? That would have been a crime." Matthew held out his hand. "Let me see."

Hesitantly she placed her foot into his hands. The electricity that flowed through them brought a flush to her face.

He leaned over to inspect her sole. As he looked, a lock of chestnut hair fell forward, almost into his eye.

"I don't see anything. It's just a little red. Your foot's cold, though. How about a special Carter foot rub? I'll do this one for free. The second foot will cost you lunch."

She tried to answer him. The words wouldn't come. Instead, she reached out and touched the lock of hair that hung over his eye.

Matthew lifted his face. Their eyes met. *A girl could lose herself in the depths of that creamy mocha.* He moved closer to her.

She leaned in, anticipating the warmth of his lips on hers.

At the end of the kiss, she slowly parted her eyelids. *Just one more?* she pleaded with her eyes.

Randi found her hand entwined with Matthew's as he kissed her again.

Sliding his hand from hers, Matthew pushed himself back into his chair. He looked as if he wanted to say something. Instead, he stood.

"I'm leaving. I can't be in here with you."

"Matthew, I didn't ask you to sleep with me."

"I know. But the temptation between us may become bigger than we can control."

Her mind whirled, knowing he was right. And her heart responded with joy. He respected her, maybe even honored her, and it felt good. Really good. She hopped off the bed.

"You're right. Thank you." She grabbed his hand and led him to the door, intending to send him out of her life.

He tilted her chin and gave her a quick kiss. "Good night." And then he was gone.

Randi rested her head against the door and fought the urge to throw it open and go after him. What was it about this man that had managed to unlock the door she had tightly bolted?

৯

Randi cradled the phone to her ear. Shopping with Pat made her long for Jess's company even more. She'd called, taking a chance on waking her to tell her about her evening with Matthew. Such ninth-grade behavior, but just what she needed. "So what do you think?"

"He's a keeper, Randi."

"Just not for me. He'll make someone a good husband." She twisted the edge of the comforter between her fingers.

"I think he might be the one for you." Jess fell silent.

"But it's not what I planned." What was that whine in her voice? She sounded like Emma.

"You can plan all you want, Randi, but God already did all the work for you. Just let Him lead you."

"So what happened to free will?" She heard ice clicking against a glass.

"It's there, but why take the hardest route?"

"What if I don't choose Matthew?" Randi couldn't stop the sudden image of Matthew, three little girls, and a puppy romping across a pasture. And she wasn't with them.

"What if you do?"

"Okay, so then I get a family? And the pain that goes with losing them?"

"What about the pain of never having them?"

Randi felt the tension in her neck travel down her spine. Why did all of this have to be so hard? "So if I don't do what God wants me to do, I'll be punished? Is that what you're telling me?"

"Back up—who said that? I just asked if you would be able to live with yourself if you sent Matthew away. Besides, God works everything together for those who love Him."

"But does He really love—"

"Don't say it, Randi. I know how you feel, or say you do. God loves you. He loves you enough to go around and through your stubbornness. I know you think He's too busy to bother with you, but He's not. He's there all the time, anytime you need Him. Even when you say you don't." Jess sighed. "So think about it, will you? God's plan for Matthew could include you."

Randi's ear burned from the cell phone. She didn't know how to respond, but her thoughts were confused. How could Matthew love her? She wasn't preacher wife material. Wouldn't God want that for him?

"I have other news for you." Jess's voice sparkled. "I'm cleared."

"Cleared?" Randi asked. "For takeoff?"

Jess laughed. "No. To come back. I called Dana, and next week we'll be back on the road together."

"Does Matthew know?" She knew he didn't know, or he would have said something.

"I'm sure Dana has a plan. I thought you didn't care."

"He'll be heartbroken."

"Sounds like you do care."

"I guess I do." Randi blinked back tears, surprised by the sadness she felt.

৯

Randi lay on the bed in the dark room, unable to sleep. The room felt void of fresh air. And the quiet. . .everything was so still she could hear the sound of her own breath going in and out. That and Jess's words. Even if she didn't want to think God had time for her, she could believe He would make time for Matthew.

She kicked the heavy bedspread off her legs and crawled out of bed. *Is Matthew finding it difficult to sleep tonight, too?* She slid the room-darkening curtains open, blinded for a moment by the bright lights of the gas station below. She watched a family of four climb out of a minivan.

What would it be like to travel with children across the States? She would like that, teaching them the history of the country. Showing them all the places she had been as a driver.

She gave herself a mental shake. A reality check was in order. There wouldn't be any traveling with children, especially her own. She grasped the edges of the curtains and yanked them shut. Darkness engulfed her as hot tears streamed down her cheeks. Could Jess be right? All she needed to do was follow God's nudges? Ask Him to lead her? It couldn't be that easy. Emma prayed all the time. So did her mother, and look at what their lives were like. *But they're happy, and I'm not.*

twenty

Matthew whistled a popular Christian song as he crossed the empty motel lobby. He couldn't find it in himself to be angry about the way Randi's fiancé had treated her. Sure, he didn't like that she'd been hurt, but if it had saved her for him, then he was okay with that.

Randi liked him, and that felt good, mighty good. The warm night air clung to him like a mother's hug as he strode across the paved parking lot to the truck. His mind raced with the possibilities of a life with Randi, and maybe Emma. He didn't mind. He'd take all of Randi's family, including the brother in jail, if it meant a future with her.

He climbed into his bunk and tried to stretch full length, but his feet hit the wall. He rolled over and bent his knees. He closed his eyes then opened them when sleep refused to come. He couldn't lie still, not when he could still feel Randi in his arms. He crawled out of the bed. He needed a snack. That would help.

Outside the truck, he glanced at Randi's window, hoping for a light. *Maybe she can't sleep, either,* he thought. If not, he'd go back up and get her. They could get the ice cream they had forgotten about earlier. The window remained dark. He frowned. Maybe she didn't have the same confusing feelings he was experiencing.

The white twinkle lights around the old-fashioned posts gave the town a movie set feel. Soft sounds of music echoed against the empty shops through the still night air. The crowds in the streets had thinned to a mere stream. Several high school–age kids were sweeping the streets, and a few

136

were lugging clear trash bags full of cans. The festival hadn't officially closed. Maybe he would find an open vendor. A funnel cake with a cup of decaf coffee would be nice. The first row of vendors he came to had closed their makeshift canvas doors over their serving counters.

Matthew stopped one of the can haulers. "Is anyone still open? I'm looking for something sweet to eat."

The girl pointed toward the sound of the music. "The ones closest to the band are, but not for long. Most of them are serving beer."

"Thanks. I'll check. Maybe someone has food left."

The tent where Matthew bought their dinner still remained open. He purchased his coffee and dessert then wandered back to where he and Randi had sat earlier.

He popped a piece of fried dough sprinkled with powdered sugar into his mouth while he watched the couples dancing. The ones who were left were older, about his parents' age. They looked as if they had been dance partners for life. Every move seemed coordinated to perfection. His heart ached with longing.

Matthew began a silent dialogue. *Father, I want that. I want a love so strong no one can look at us and say we made a mistake. If it's Randi You've chosen for me, please show me how to bring her to You. I've tried talking to her, but I don't think I'm getting anywhere. Oh, I know, Father, any word spoken about You is never wasted. But sometimes. . .sometimes I feel like she's bricked herself into a soundproof room. Amen.*

He brushed the powdered sugar off his jeans then added to his prayer. *Father, can You answer this one faster than the last big request I had? She's beautiful, and if she's not for me, please move me somewhere I can't see her every day.*

twenty-one

With her backpack slung over her shoulder, Randi trotted through the lobby and out the door. She reached the truck huffing and leaned on the door with one hand. With a tight fist, she banged against the metal to warn Matthew of her impending entrance. She retrieved her key from her jeans pocket, inserted it into the lock, and turned. As the door opened, its hinges grated, matching the growl of her stomach that reminded her she should eat.

"I'm driving first," she called. The curtain was drawn tight across the sleeping area. She didn't hear a response. With both hands she yanked the canvas curtain across the rod.

He wasn't asleep. He wasn't even there. His Bible, cell phone, and guitar rested on his bunk, but not him.

She flung her backpack into the corner. *Where is he?* She didn't think she'd passed him in the lobby. It didn't matter if she did; he'd find out she had checked out. No doubt he would return in a few minutes.

And next week Jess will be back! She sighed with relief. After last night, the sooner she and Matthew parted, the better.

Despite the conversation with Jess, Randi knew Matthew couldn't be part of God's greater plan for her. Why would he be? If anyone, Emma should come before Matthew.

And yet I've denied her a home with me. She crashed onto the lower bunk. She had done just that, refused to take a little girl who loved her into her home. She wasn't any better than her brother. It didn't matter that Emma wasn't her child. She'd stood there in church and accepted the responsibility of being her godmother, praying for her, taking care of her in case her brother couldn't or wouldn't. She hadn't done any of it.

The gravity of what she'd left undone hit her in the chest. She gasped for breath. *I am so sorry, Emma.* But what could she do? Nothing had changed, other than her guilt had been left behind and replaced with sorrow. Changes had to be made. But first she had to get home, and that couldn't happen until Matthew returned. She couldn't very well leave him behind—again. Not when he'd been so understanding about her log book.

But he'd better get back soon. It's not like he had access to a shower this morning. Maybe she should go look for him. He wouldn't have gone far. He had to know she would be ready to leave early, eager to make up the time they missed yesterday. She sat up and flipped on the CD player. Sounds of Ben Glover's "26 Letters" poured through the cab. Matthew's music. She considered changing it but decided she liked the sound and left it alone.

She moved to the back and straightened the bunk. She picked up the pillow and sniffed. It smelled like him. She closed her eyes, remembering his kisses. *Enough! It's over, remember?* She shoved the pillow into the corner.

Back in the front, she switched out the CD for some blues. Where could Matthew be? Aggravated that he still hadn't returned, she grabbed a pen and pad of paper from the cubby at the front of the cab.

M.

   Came early so we could leave. You're missing so I went to the bakery down the street. Find me there.

                                                    R.

She ripped the yellow note from the pad and stuck it to the steering wheel. She hoped he wouldn't climb in on the passenger's side and miss it. She didn't have time for a comedy routine of the two of them just missing each other all morning.

She slammed the door behind her. A thick gray cloud sneaked over the sun as she walked down the street. A Danish and coffee would taste good. The small town seemed silent after last night's revelry. The booths still stood, vacant and eerily ghostlike this morning. The streets showed no signs of the crowd that had been here the night before.

As she approached the bakery, she stopped and stared. A line appeared to have grown from the front door. Randi groaned. She hadn't expected to have to wait. She looked again. It wasn't a line, but a group. What could be so exciting at a bakery this early in the morning? It seemed to be a quiet group. She could only hear one voice.

A familiar voice. *Matthew.*

Anger bubbled inside her throat as she grasped at a reason to be mad at him. How could he? How could he make her wait while he played teacher to a bunch of believers? Well, she would take care of that. After all, he wasn't hired to preach to the multitudes. He was hired to take care of his fellow truckers, and these people didn't qualify just because some of them drove pickups. She elbowed her way through the crowd until she stood next to him.

She shook his arm. "Matthew. We need to leave. Now."

"Randi. Meet some of my new friends."

"Hi." Randi stretched her lips into a counterfeit smile. "I've been waiting for you. You could have left me a note or something," she hissed at him.

"I'm sorry. I didn't realize I'd been here so long. I came down to get us breakfast and started talking to a few people, and before I knew it I was teaching a small Bible class about Paul."

"Glad you enjoyed yourself." She smiled at the group. "I'm sorry, but *Teach* needs to get back on the road."

"Let us know the next time you're going to be close enough for us to drive, Matthew. We'll come to the nearest truck stop to hear you preach," said a voice in the back.

"I'll need a phone number from one of you. The rest of you get your name on a call list."

"Joe, you make the call list. You can do them on that spreadsheet you love, like you do for your soccer team." Loud snickers wafted among the men.

"Sure, I'll handle it, or rather my wife will. She's the one who puts those lists together, not me," Joe said. He handed Matthew a business card. "My number is at the bottom. Hope you get by here again soon."

"I hope so, too."

Randi couldn't believe the glow that seemed to radiate from Matthew's face. He really believed the stuff he taught.

"Matthew, we have to go." Randi stood with her arms crossed and glared at him. She moved to the side while the group of listeners dispersed with cups in their hands.

"I'm almost ready. I want to get us some breakfast before we leave if that's okay. Isn't that why you're here?"

"Not exactly. You weren't where you were supposed to be, and I grew tired of waiting. I thought I might as well eat." Randi pulled a wad of dollars from her jeans pocket and thrust the money at him.

Matthew waved it away. "No, I'll get it." He turned away from her and walked to the counter and placed their order.

"You want me to drive?" Matthew asked, interrupting her thoughts.

"No. I didn't drive at all yesterday."

Matthew held out a small white paper sack. She took it, mumbling her thanks before walking out the door. She took small sips of the hot coffee while Matthew walked next to her. Neither spoke until they were back at the SLEEP-INN.

Matthew brushed against her arm. "Are you okay?"

"Why?" She followed him between a Mustang and the minivan she'd seen pull in last night. *They must be sleeping in this morning or letting the kids work off some energy in the pool before the rest of their drive.*

"Because last night I thought. . ."

She stopped short, realizing what he was talking about.

"You thought what? One kiss and everything would be like a fairy tale?"

He turned to face her. "Not exactly. But you did kiss me back. I couldn't help but think perhaps you might like me enough not to yell first thing in the morning."

She could see the pain in his eyes. Did he think she was like that girl in college? She hadn't wanted to hurt him. "Well, if that's all you were expecting, I suppose I could keep the conversation friendly."

As they came to the front of the truck, her stomach rolled. "I didn't do the pre-check."

"No problem. I'll run through it for you."

"Sure." Randi shivered, thinking about what Matthew didn't know. She almost drove off this morning without checking over the load. If he had been sleeping, she would have left without thinking about it. She shook the feeling of doom from her shoulders. The chance of something being wrong the first and only time she had forgotten had to be small. *But something could have.* How many times had they drilled the importance of the pre-check into them in school? It was supposed to be as automatic as putting the toothbrush in your mouth every morning.

"Checks out fine. There's still enough reefer fuel to make it to the next stop." Matthew stood looking at her. "Something wrong? You've been standing there like that since we got here."

"No, it's nothing. Let's just go." She opened the door, climbed up, and plucked the note she had left for Matthew from the wheel. She crunched it and jammed it into the bag she kept for trash.

Inside, Matthew grabbed his Bible and a notebook before buckling himself into the passenger seat. "I had a great idea for a sermon back at the bakery and need to get it down so I don't forget it."

"Good for you." Through the windshield the summer sky dimmed, and navy blue and black took its place.

"I'm sorry I wasn't here when you came down, Randi. I thought I would have at least half an hour before you woke. It's still early. We haven't lost any time this morning."

"No, but who knows, we may end up behind an accident now instead of in front of one." Lightning streaked horizontally, leaving jagged white line etchings in her eyes.

"Or maybe God is protecting us from one that we might have been involved in if we had left earlier," Matthew said.

She let that pass, knowing that even though he had already taught one class this morning, he would enjoy giving her a private lesson. Maybe distraction would work. "I told Emma you would take her to your farm."

"You did?" The look he gave her was unreadable.

"If you'd rather we didn't come. . ."

"No, I want you to come. I wanted to ask you before."

"But you didn't."

"I know. My mom would have thought we were dating."

"We're not dating." This wasn't the kind of distraction she wanted. "It was one night and a few kisses. That's it." She thought fast. "Besides, I wouldn't make a good pastor's wife, and you know it."

He closed his Bible with a snap. "I haven't asked you to marry me."

That hurt in a way she didn't think possible. Before she had time to process if she would need stitches, a gust of wind battered the trailer, yanking the wheel from her hands. She quickly caught it, clutching it tight. She squeezed her biceps until she thought they would pop free of her skin. Just as she risked a glance at the side mirror, another blast rammed them. The back of the trailer lifted.

"What can I do?" Matthew asked.

"Nothing," she said through gritted teeth. "Pray?" She felt the back end fishtail. Like hot tar, the shoulder of the road sucked at her wheels. *Don't overcorrect! Take your time.* The instructions she'd learned came back to her as she wrestled with the rig, hating the sound of gravel urging her to panic.

On the other side of the interstate, the wind caught another driver. She gasped as she saw the back of his trailer lift two feet. It landed on the shoulder. The back of the trailer started to slide toward the front; then the truck jackknifed. Its cab skated across the pavement toward the median.

Then the rain came, not in soft spatters but in thick waves, bringing another slap from the wind.

"There's a message from dispatch on the Qualcomm." Matthew pointed at the red light.

"I can't play with them right now. I'm learning to windsurf." Her voice felt as tight as the tension in her shoulders. "So find out what they want."

He didn't say anything. The suspense grated her already-raw nerves. She glanced over at him. The expression on his face told her she wouldn't like what the message said.

"What's wrong?" Another gust moved the trailer onto the shoulder. The wind pummeled them as Randi tried to keep them centered between two lanes.

"Your mom is in the hospital, and they want you to come get Emma."

twenty-two

They'd dropped their load and asked Dana for permission to turn and burn. The only time they stopped was to switch drivers, refuel, and grab sandwiches. They rolled into the Round the Clock yard and dropped the truck. Randi drove straight to the hospital, followed by Matthew in his truck.

At the hospital, Randi welcomed the pressure of Matthew's hand in hers. He'd insisted on coming with her. It would have been impossible for her to sit and do nothing while she worried.

Dr. Sommer calmly stuffed his hand into the pocket of his lab coat as if he hadn't just tossed a live grenade into her life.

"What do you mean, she's not coming home?"

"I find it's best for a patient this age to recover in an assisted care facility. A broken hip and leg requires twenty-four-hour nursing followed by therapy. Those bones are not going to heal quickly." He averted his eyes, and she wondered how many times a week, or a day, he delivered news like this.

"The nurse will help you place her." Before she could protest, his beeper sounded. With an apologetic look he said, "We'll talk later," and hustled down the hall.

"Matthew, I—"

"Miss Bell?"

Randi turned. A short, twentysomething woman pranced down the hallway. Her bright, flounced skirt bounced above her sensible black pumps. A red leather briefcase hung from her shoulder. She looked familiar.

She pressed a card into Randi's hand. "Kate Trent, social services. We've met before. I'm here about Emma."

"Where is she?" Randi felt like she was trapped in Tom's Twister. The carnival ride spun fast, plastering her to its wall; then the floor fell two feet, leaving her hanging in the air. She wanted off.

Kate wore a stern look, amplified by the black frame glasses perched on her nose. "Emma will be here in a minute. She's having a snack. Now before she gets here, I need to know what you plan to do with her."

"Do with her?" Like a parrot, Randi repeated the question. Emma came around the corner, carrying a candy bar.

"She has to go with you, or I have to put her in foster care."

"No! I won't go!" Emma tossed her candy bar and scurried to Randi, wailing like a wounded animal.

Randi bent down, gathered her into her arms, and rocked her back and forth. "Shh, Emma. It's going to be okay." She met Matthew's eyes, silently begging him to tell her how it possibly could.

❧

Randi tucked Emma into bed and kissed her good night.

"Will you listen to my good-night prayer, like Grandma?"

"It's been a long day, kid, and I'm not very good at prayers. Matthew's still here. Do you want me to get him?"

Emma turned away from her and faced the wall. "No."

"Emma, come on, it's late."

"It's okay. You don't have to listen. God will." Emma flipped around. Her eyes gleamed with fresh tears. "But it's better if you're here."

"Let's hear it, then." Randi folded her hands like she'd been taught years ago in Sunday school.

"Dear God, please make Grandma Bell better. Please remember Daddy. He's sorry for what he did, God. He asked me to forgive him for losing our home and I did, just like You said we should. Amen." She huddled into a ball under the covers. "Good night, Aunt Randi."

"Sweet dreams, pumpkin." Randi traced Emma's cheek then turned off the lamp, pausing at the doorway as she heard Emma murmur.

"God, thank You for answering my prayer."

Randi's feet turned to stone and she froze, unsure what to do. Had He really given Emma an answer to something?

". . .making Aunt Randi my mom."

Emma's new mom? The words pricked a small fault in Randi's protective shell. The crack radiated like a web in a broken windshield, but didn't break. She closed the bedroom door.

In the kitchen, Matthew waited for her with steaming hot chocolate in a rainbow mug. She quirked her eyebrow as she slid into the chair. "How did you know this is my comfort cup?"

"I didn't. Just seemed like a good size. The other ones aren't big enough to add the powder to the hot water and have room to stir."

The phone on the wall rang. Randi thrust the chair backward and dove for the phone. *The hospital?* Her heart raced as she answered it.

"Randi, I just heard about your mom. Is there anything I can do?" Jess's concerned voice came through the line.

"No, nothing right now." To Matthew she whispered, "It's not the hospital; it's Jess."

"Who's with you?"

"Matthew came back with Emma and me. So you know Mom broke a hip and a leg?"

"How long until she can come home?"

"She's not, at least not for weeks. She has to go to one of those assisted living centers. I'm taking care of Emma for now. When are you coming back to drive?"

"About that." Jess sighed. "There isn't an easy way to tell you."

Randi's stomach turned. "The day can't get any worse, Jess. Just say it."

"Mike and I are engaged."

"That's great, Jess! Good news, not bad."

"There's more. He wants to get married next month and asked me to quit driving. He wants to start a family."

"But we're partners." Randi hated the pleading tone in her voice, but if that was what it took. . .

"We were. But we never said we'd do this forever, Randi. Remember, it was supposed to be until we found our Prince Charming and decided to live happily ever after."

Randi swallowed. *Prince Charming? Happily ever after?* She didn't think that had been a serious goal when she agreed to it.

Jess continued, "I've found mine, and I think you may have found yours."

Randi noticed Matthew trying not to eavesdrop. An impossible task in this tiny kitchen. She couldn't talk about Prince Charming now, not with him in the kitchen. "Jess, I'm really tired. I'll call you tomorrow."

She hung up the phone. "Jess isn't coming back to drive. If Dana will let us keep driving together, I'll be able to take care of Emma until Mom comes home."

Matthew frowned then looked down at his cup. "I told Dana I couldn't ride with you anymore."

"What? Why? Because of a few kisses?"

He pushed back his chair and gave her an intense look she didn't understand.

"Yeah, that's it." He turned and put his cup in the sink. "It's late. I'd better be going. I'll call you."

As soon as the door closed, Randi leaned against it and let loose the tears she'd held back all day. *If You really are listening, God, I need You.*

a&

Randi dragged herself to her mother's room. She collapsed on the bed and curled into a ball. Tears flowed, and she smothered her sobs with a pillow. She told God about the guilt she carried and the fears of being responsible for Emma. She felt His hands reach out for her. And then she knew as she placed her hand in His, He'd been with her all along. He'd been there when the kids made fun of her, when her dad disappeared, and He'd even been with her the day she'd found Brent with the Realtor. She'd called Him TV Dad. The dad she'd always wanted, one who would be there anytime she needed Him. Did A.J. know that's who He was? She'd ask Emma.

Before breakfast, Emma crawled in bed with her. Randi slipped her arm around the little girl.

"Emma, last night you told God you've forgiven your dad. What did you mean?"

Emma snuggled closer to her. "Dad said he was sorry he couldn't be a real dad anymore because he has to be in jail for a long time. But he said he loves me, and he's going to ask you to adopt me because you'll be a good mom."

"And you forgave him, just like that?"

"Nope. I was mad. But at Sunday school I learned that God wants me to forgive Dad. That's why Jesus came, so everybody could forgive. I'm not sure how it works, but I felt better when I decided not to be mad anymore."

"You're a good daughter." Randi wasn't quite sure she could so easily forgive A.J. Did he know how fortunate he was that his daughter had forgiven him? Randi couldn't forgive him, not yet. But she would honor his request and adopt Emma. She'd begun praying about that, but it would take time—and God. At least that's what Jess had said. God can do it right now, but you have to choose to let Him. Free choice. It made life so much harder when you bumbled around making the wrong decisions.

twenty-three

As they crossed through the rough field, Randi clung to Matthew's hand, and he noticed how small her fingers were next to his.

"Are we close?" Randi asked. "I don't see anything but never-ending fields."

"Not much farther." Matthew squeezed her hand.

"There really is a creek? Shouldn't there be trees around it?" She raised her hand to her forehead to shield her eyes from the sun and peered into the distance.

"There are. You just can't see them yet. Be patient. At least you aren't carrying this heavy basket." He leaned to one side to prove it weighed enough to keep him unbalanced.

"Ouch!" Randi stooped and picked at one of the tiny burrs embedded between her sock and shoe.

He watched her remove a few more. "You know you'll get more on the way back, don't you?"

She glared at him and stood. "This better be worth the trouble."

They came to the crest of the hill. Matthew set the basket on the ground. He maneuvered Randi in front of him.

"Look, Randi. See those trees? That's where the creek is, and where we can finally sit and talk."

"I can't wait." She turned and grinned. She reached her arms around his neck, tilted her head, and kissed him gently on the lips. Her eyes enticed him with their colors of blue and green. "Want to race?"

He didn't answer her but took off running, his heart racing, not from the exertion but from the excitement of love.

Randi raced after him, laughing.

"Not fair." She crashed down next to him on the creek bank. "You have longer legs."

"You ran? I had time to spread the blanket." He gestured to the rumpled mess under him.

"More like you dropped it on the ground and sat on it only seconds before I got here." She pointed at him. "Up, Preacher Man. Let me spread that so we can both sit on it."

Preacher Man? Now that was a handle he liked. He stood and grabbed a corner of the blanket and helped her smooth it. Sitting across from her, he unwrapped the sandwiches and handed her one. He raised his turkey sandwich to his lips.

Randi's eyes widened. "Aren't you going to pray first?"

"Almost forgot," he said, embarrassed. "Not good for a pastor, is it?"

"I'll say it, since you've forgotten how."

Matthew watched in stunned silence as Randi placed her lunch on her lap, closed her eyes, and folded her hands.

After the prayer, she reached out and touched his hand. "There's something else I need to tell you."

"Like you hate picnics?" He started to take a bite.

"This is serious, Matthew. You promise you won't say 'I told you so' or laugh?"

Matthew felt his breathing slow, and he put the sandwich down. Serious couldn't be good. "Okay."

She cocked her head at him and lifted an eyebrow.

"I promise." He put a hand over his heart for emphasis.

"I get it. I mean, I get that God loves me and He does listen to everything. I've even been asking Him for help."

"I would never laugh at you for asking for God's help." Matthew's lips lifted into a smile. "Why would you think I would?"

"Maybe not laugh, but get that satisfied grin on your face."

"Can't help it." The smile on his face grew into a huge grin.

"So has He helped you?"

"Let's see—Dana is letting me out of my contract, and your mom is watching Emma." Excitement almost made her jump up and down like a child, but she decided she'd probably break an ankle if she did that. "And I got the teaching job. Too bad it took me so long to find Him. I wasted a lot of time." Randi took a bite of her sandwich.

"So what brought all this change, Randi?" Matthew brushed an ant from the blanket.

"The night you said you wouldn't ride with me anymore." She looked away for a moment then whispered, "Then you left."

More than anything he wanted to hug away the hurt etched on her face. He wanted to, but he didn't. A small voice told him she needed to say it all.

She took a breath. "I felt abandoned. First my dad, then my brother became undependable, and then my fiancé, even God, I thought. I gave up. But then you came along, and I thought you were different." Tears rolled down her face, and she sniffed.

This was one of those times he wished he could whip a handkerchief from a pocket like the men in those old movies his mom watched. Instead, he reached into the basket for a napkin and held it out to her.

She took it and blew her nose. "Sorry. I didn't think I would cry."

"That's okay, but you have to tell me the rest of the story."

"I don't know if I can explain it. I was crying, and I remember asking God if He was listening. It's weird, but in my mind I saw Him standing in a boat and offering me His hand. Then I knew. All this time, He was TV Dad."

"Huh?"

"Crazy, I know. TV Dad started out being someone A.J. and I pretended was our real dad. We knew it was the church dropping off gifts at Christmas, but we wanted to feel loved by a dad. Now I realize TV Dad for me was really my true Father, and He's always been there for me."

"Are you telling me that you believe in God, that He loves you enough to have sent His Son to die in your place?" Excitement charged through Matthew's heart.

"Yes. I always did believe in God, but I felt like He didn't care about me. I was wrong. He cared about me every second of my life. I was just too stubborn to see that."

"I'm glad. Glad that you found your way back to Him." *Thank You, God, for an answered prayer.*

"Mom and Jess were praying for me, and lately Emma, too."

"And me, Randi." Matthew slid his arms around her shoulders, pulling her close. He felt nothing but love for this woman as he kissed her.

"Marry me, Randi, please. I want more than a kiss here and there. I want to go to sleep next to you at night, be the father of your children, go on vacations together, and worship with you."

Her eyes seemed to dance with joy; then her face grew serious. "Can you give up driving?"

Matthew felt as if ice water had been dumped down his back. This was the woman he'd felt sure God wanted him to love. She couldn't be asking him to give up what he'd been called for, could she? He pulled away from her. "I can't."

"Sure you can."

A cow mooed in the pasture somewhere behind him. Devastated, Matthew felt the trap of his youth squeeze him. His dad's offer to work the farm with him roamed through his mind, but he couldn't be a farmer, not even for Randi.

"Only when you pry my stone-cold fingers from the steering wheel."

"Then I can't marry you. I've seen too many marriages ruined in this business."

"But, Randi, this is what I've been called to do." Matthew

knew God had answered part of his prayer, too. But was he ready to give up his dream of traveling across the country?

"I know, but I've been called to be Emma's mother." Randi began flinging the sandwiches back into the basket. "I think it's best if you take me home."

She tried to hide them from him, but he saw her blink back the tears before she hid her face. Still, he couldn't do want she wanted; he just couldn't.

twenty-four

A few weeks later, Randi held open the door of her new home and embraced her best friend. "Jess, I'm glad you came."

Jess removed her sunglasses and entered the house. "It *is* small. I thought you were exaggerating when you said it wasn't much bigger than the sleep cab."

Randi eyed the room. "It doesn't look too bad, does it?" The corner shelf unit held books, Barbie dolls, and cows, which had become Emma's new hobby after she'd found a ceramic one at the thrift shop. The new couch hugged one wall, and the television sat in the other corner on top of an old trunk. "It's nice to have a garage and a backyard. But the bonus—"

"No trash bin outside your door." Jess finished the sentence for her. "It looks nice, Randi. I love the pictures on the wall." Jess walked over for a closer look. "These are new. From Matthew's farm?"

"Cows gave it away?" Randi laughed. "Emma loves the cows and Matthew's mom."

Jess sank into the couch with a puzzled look. "Doesn't she love Matthew, too?"

"He's not around much, but when he is, yes, she does," Randi said with dissatisfaction in her voice. "How did the interview with the florist go?"

"Still can't decide on my bouquet. Roses or daisies?"

Randi wondered if she would ever experience a walk down the aisle, much less a ring with a diamond that size on her finger. "You'll figure it out. I made tea. Would you like some?"

"Sure." Jess popped off the couch. "I'll come with you.

155

I want to see the kitchen. Can you really touch both walls at the same time?"

"Almost," Randi said as she led Jess into the galley-sized room.

Randi laughed at the expression on Jess's face when she turned around.

"You weren't kidding."

"We don't need a lot of space." Randi poured a glass of iced tea and handed it to Jess. Picking up her glass, she said, "It will take less than five seconds to see the rest of the place."

After the tour, Jess settled on the couch once again and asked, "Any change in Matthew?"

Randi set her glass on the coffee table. "No. He's still insisting he can drive and be a good husband and parent. I don't know, Jess. I'm having trouble sticking to my decision."

"You don't love him enough to give in on letting him drive?" Jess sank back farther into the couch and slid off her shoes.

"I have to think of Emma and any other children we might have. I look into the future and see me, frazzled from taking care of the kids for days. Matthew will come home, and I'll fly out the door to experience some kind of life. He won't want to get a babysitter because he'll have been away from them all week."

"So now you can see into the future? Why don't you let God take care of what will happen? If you love Matthew, you have to trust things will turn out the right way."

"I'm not ready to do that. There has to be a way for this to work. I don't want to be a single mom while he's gone so much. I'm doing that now, and it's harder than I thought."

Jess leaned forward. "Are you sorry you adopted Emma?"

"No. Not at all. I'm grateful every morning when I wake up and realize she's in the room next to me. I just want—no, need—a husband who's here to love them, play with them, and assemble toys."

"Assemble toys?" Jess looked at her with a frown.

"Just wait. Barbie's mansion is a nightmare to put together."

"How many houses can Barbie have?"

"It's not that, not really. I want a normal family life. I want to have dinner on the table and have a husband to feed. I want to wake up every morning next to Matthew. I want to be disgusted by clothes on the closet floor." Randi squeezed her eyes tight for a minute to stop tears that threatened to spill. "I want a marriage."

ea

An envelope with a return address from Blessed Savior Church sat on top of Matthew's mail. He ripped it open and pulled out the letter.

Dear Mr. Carter,

Blessed Savior Church has been made aware of you through one of our members. We are interested in talking to you about starting a ministry at our local truck stop on a permanent basis. If you would be interested in discussing this further with us, please call.

He shook his head in disbelief. "Who could have given them my name?"

Matthew paced the kitchen. "Tied down, that's what I'd be. Stuck in one town forever. But I could still work with the truckers. . . . No, I can't. I just can't give up the road." He shoved the letter into his pocket. Unable to think, he left the house.

Hot and sweating from the exertion of trying to walk away his thoughts, he stopped at the end of the pasture. He wiped the moisture from his face with his shirttail then tramped along the creek bank until he came to his spot. He'd come here to make major decisions since he was old enough to escape his mother. Decisions about what car to buy, whether he would go to prom, where to go to school, and even whether to drive a truck or take over the farm for his dad.

That's the problem. He didn't want to live in one small town forever. Too many towns remained out there for him to explore—for him to preach the gospel in. He wanted the life of the apostles.

Matthew climbed into his tree and crawled out onto the branch that hung over the creek. The water whispered as it raced by. His thoughts kept pace with the rush. He pulled the crumpled letter from his shirt pocket and spread it on the branch before him.

An answer to a prayer, right, Father? But it wasn't the answer he wanted. He'd spent nights asking God how he could marry Randi. He didn't contemplate even for a moment that the answer might mean that to make it work he had to give up his dream.

Too much to ask. He'd worked too hard to become a driver, to have the chance to see the world. He balled the paper into his fist, pulled his hand back, and aimed at the creek. At the point of letting go, he changed his mind and stuck it into his pocket. If only he didn't love her so much, he could walk away. But he *did* love her. Was he man enough to give up his dream for her?

He spent an hour in prayer asking for guidance. Stiff from lying on the branch, he lowered himself, hanging from the branch before he dropped. He landed on his backside. *Funny, that never happened before. Kick in the pants from God?* He stood and brushed the dirt from the back of his jeans. *There is still time to work this out,* he thought. He needed to spend more time in prayer on this one. Meanwhile, he'd see Randi and Emma when he could. They would have to understand.

twenty-five

Saturday afternoon Randi slowed the car as she drove through the rest stop. The sunshine danced through the window, its warmth belying the fact that it would soon be October and snow would soon fall. She looked for Matthew's truck. Spotting it, she zipped into a parking spot just past it. She checked in the mirror to see how she looked. Her hair, now cut short, would be a surprise to him. But it looked so much better and she wanted a more professional style that was easier to maintain now that she was teaching.

Someone tapped on her window. She looked up to see Matthew posed there with a big grin on his face.

She opened her door and jumped out. "Hi," she said, feeling shy about her new appearance.

"I saw you pull off the interstate." Matthew reached up and skimmed his fingers along the bottom of her hair. "You cut it," he said.

"I had to, to survive. Getting both Emma's hair and mine done takes more time than I ever imagined."

Matthew pulled her into his arms. "You look great. I like short," he whispered into her ear. He continued to hold her. "I've missed you so much."

"I've missed you, too, Preacher Man." She reached up and kissed him gently on the lips. She had missed him these past few weeks. Phone calls could warm you on the inside, but nothing could replace a hug from the person you loved.

"I didn't expect you to be alone. I thought Emma was coming."

"She has a new friend, Jenny, who asked her to spend the day with her. She thought that would be more fun than coming with me." She heard Matthew's stomach growl. "Hungry? I brought a picnic lunch."

"You cooked?"

She almost laughed at the disbelief on his face. "No. But I put the meat between slices of wheat bread." She grinned at him. "I even brought some of those big pickles you like so much." She reached into the car and grabbed a brown sack.

"What, no basket? Not very romantic, are you?" Matthew teased.

"Hey, you should be grateful I was able to assemble a lunch with my morning routine." She gave him a playful shove and walked toward the covered picnic tables, glancing over her shoulder to make sure he followed. Only a few colored leaves clung to their branches.

Handing Matthew a sandwich, Randi decided she liked the feeling of taking care of him. "I wish I could make lunch for you every day."

Matthew didn't eat it, though. Sitting on the bench, he just held it and stared at her for a moment. Then he drew a deep breath.

"Randi, please marry me. Being apart from you doesn't feel right." Matthew reached out and grasped her hand tightly.

Her heart beat faster. She plopped down beside him and squeezed his hand. "I want that, too, but unless you give up driving, I can't marry you." She wouldn't let tears fall from her eyes. She wouldn't. She blinked faster.

"Why? Tell me why this can't work for us. Other men manage a marriage and keep driving."

"Temptation, Matthew. I'm talking about temptation. It's happened to me before, and Brent wasn't a trucker. You're even more at risk. I won't go through it again." She looked him in the eye and squeezed his hand. "It's just too easy to fall into someone else's arms if your husband or wife isn't around enough. People will reach for comfort when they need it."

"But if we both cling to God and look to Him for all comfort—"

"I know, Matthew, but we aren't perfect. We can fall into sin."

"So you're not willing to take a chance that I can be faithful to you while I'm on the road?" Matthew set his sandwich down on the paper plate Randi had brought. "I don't know how to prove to you that I love you enough never to endanger our marriage."

"How can you be so sure? There are plenty of female truckers who need counseling. A few tears, a hug, and before you know it, there might be chemistry between the two of you."

"So what do you want from me, Randi?"

"Find a job here so we'll be together every night."

"I don't think I can do that. I told you I didn't want to be stuck in one town the rest of my life. If I do that, I might as well go back and work on the farm." Matthew's face was downcast as he avoided looking at her.

"Then I guess there isn't anything else to discuss. I love you, Matthew, but Emma needs me."

"Come with me. Work by my side," Matthew pleaded.

"And Emma? I want to be there for her—every day." Randi withdrew her hand from his. "It's not like I don't miss driving, too, Matthew. But my life changed, and I'm glad."

"Don't give up driving, then; bring her. Other families do it. You can homeschool her."

"No. That's not a life for her. She's been uprooted enough. She needs a home, a school with friends, maybe a dog. I've spent a lot of time thinking about this. I can't do what you're asking."

"Where does that leave us, then? Do we throw away our feelings and just move on?"

Heartsick, she could hardly force the words from her constricted throat. "Sounds that way, doesn't it?"

"But I love you."

"Not enough to let go of your dream." Randi stood. She brushed the tears from her cheeks, wishing she was important enough to him that he would be willing to give up anything for her. "I love you, Matthew. I always will. But I guess this wasn't meant to be after all."

Before he could say anything else, she turned and ran toward her car in the truck parking lot.

❧

Matthew's heart ached as he watched Randi's car pull out of her spot. No longer hungry, he gathered his sandwich, plate, and napkin and shoved them into the paper bag. He sat for a moment, thinking about what had happened and how it had happened so fast.

He smashed the bag of lunch and tossed it into the trash bin. He didn't even try to save it for later. He had lost a treasure.

A gift God sent me.

He knew he could have the gift back, *if* he gave up something dear to his heart. *Gain one, lose one.* How could he? He didn't want to choose. God had called him to reach out to others, hadn't He? Wasn't he supposed to give up all and follow God, just like the disciples?

His conscience nagged at him. If that was true, shouldn't he be happy about his choice? Instead, his world looked dark and joyless. He'd lost not only Randi, but Emma, too.

He walked back to the picnic table, held his head in his hands, and prayed. *Why, Father? Why can't I have it all?* He cried in silence to God for answers.

With a heavy heart and no easy solutions, he walked down the hill to his truck.

As he got closer to the parking lot, he noticed a group of people huddled together. Curious to see what was going on, he picked up his pace.

"Matthew."

He turned toward the voice and saw Brad, his partner.

"Get over here," Brad called softly. "That nutcase is here, and he's pointing a gun at Randi."

Randi? But she had left. Matthew had seen her drive off. Air left his lungs and didn't want to return. He tried to push through the group, but hands held him back. Brad stood next to him.

"We radioed the police. They'll be here in a minute."

"Let me go." Matthew pried at the hands that held him until they released him. He elbowed through the small crowd to the front.

Randi huddled next to Reb, another female driver. Randi must have seen her as she was leaving and stopped to talk. Behind them was a man holding a pistol trained on the two women. His mouth went dry as he struggled for words to call out.

What can I do, God? A plan came to him. Adrenaline propelled him back through the onlookers. He inhaled in a failed attempt to put his body in control. He found Brad. "I'm going behind the truck next to Randi and Reb and see if I can get the guy with the gun to talk to me. Maybe they'll be able to inch back to the side of Reb's truck. Think you're up to going on the other side of her truck and motioning to them if they look at you, see if you can get them to move?"

"You bet," Brad answered.

Please, God, keep us safe. Give me the words to disarm this man. Matthew raced around the back end of the trucks. He slowed his pace, but his heart continued its rapid rhythm. He walked down the side of Reb's truck. As he arrived at the front, he could hear the man's voice. He was close to Randi. Too close.

"Just tell me where I can find some trucker that goes by the name of Bingo, and I won't hurt you."

"Why do you need him?" Matthew called out. He crept

closer. "Maybe I can help you."

"Don't come any closer, or I'll shoot the women. Trash—that's all they are, anyway."

Matthew stopped walking. He wouldn't look at Randi. If he did, he knew he would lose all control of his emotions. "What's your name?"

"Doesn't matter. I just want the man who killed my wife with his truck."

Matthew took a step closer. "Can you tell me what he looks like?" He heard Randi whisper his name. He felt his gaze drifting her way. He willed himself not to look. *If anyone gets hurt today, dear God, let it be me.*

"Big guy. Wears a hat."

If he wasn't so scared, Matthew might have laughed. That described over half the truck drivers in Wyoming. "Why do you think he's here?"

"I'm checking every place trucks stop. I'm going to find him and settle this."

"If he killed your wife, why isn't he in jail?"

"The jury let him go. Said it was an accident." The man started waving his gun around. "I'll kill all of you. It doesn't matter to me who dies." The man spit a hunk of chewing tobacco onto the pavement.

"What's your name?" Matthew said.

After a moment of silence, the man said, "Al."

"Al, do you think your wife would have wanted you to take revenge like this?"

"Doesn't matter what she thinks anymore. But yeah, she would have wanted me to avenge her death."

"By shooting Randi and Reb, Al?" Matthew hated to draw attention to them, but maybe if Al saw them as women, he wouldn't shoot them.

"They're truckers. They're part of it. They might even have been in the truck with him."

The man was more out of control than Matthew thought. Surely he would have known from the trial if anyone else had been involved in the accident. Matthew grasped for anything to say that might make a difference.

"Somebody better talk soon, or I'm killing the skinny one."

Randi. Not an ounce of fat on her. *Dear Jesus, help us, please.*

"Al, her name is Randi. If you shoot her, you're going to leave a beautiful little girl without a mother. That's not what you want to do, is it? Bring grief to her precious daughter?" Matthew could see that Brad hadn't done what he had suggested. Instead, he was creeping up behind Al.

Matthew needed to distract Al so the gunman wouldn't hear Brad, but he wanted to be near enough to Randi to protect her. He took a deep breath and stepped closer to Randi.

"What are you doing? Don't go over there," Al shouted. The gun wavered in the air.

"Why not? If you're going to shoot her, I want to kiss her good-bye before she goes to heaven. Yeah, heaven—that's where she'll go. You won't kill her, Al, just her body, because she's a Christian. And I'm kissing her because I love her just like you loved your wife. I bet you'd like to have had a chance to kiss your wife good-bye, wouldn't you, Al?" Matthew tried to think of the next thing to say. He had to talk loudly to cover Brad's moves and keep Al's attention pointed at him. "Well, Al? Aren't you going to answer that question?"

"Yeah, I would have kissed her good-bye. But I didn't get the chance, and you won't, either, if you don't tell me where Bingo is." Al raised his gun hand just as Brad smacked into him, knocking him to the ground. The gun fell out of Al's hand and spun away.

Brad jumped onto Al. Several truckers rushed to help restrain the gunman as Matthew grabbed the gun.

He breathed a sigh of relief as he heard sirens in the air. Brad stood, and others took over holding Al on the ground until the police arrived.

Matthew raced to Randi and wrapped her in his arms, realizing how close he had come to losing her. What if Al had shot her? What if she had died? Could he have lived with the knowledge that his selfishness had kept him from the woman he loved? He didn't think so. But now was not the time to tell her. He knew her too well. She would think he was reacting to the emotion of the day and not to his true feelings.

"Are you all right?" He smoothed a strand of hair from her face, much like a father would do to his little girl.

"Matthew, I've never been so scared before. Even when Jess was shot. That just happened. I never saw a gun. I've never had a gun pointed at me before." Her eyes widened with every staccato sentence.

He could feel her shaking in his arms, and he held her tighter. "Everything is okay now. You don't have to be afraid. Randi, I love you so much. I almost lost you."

She pushed away from him. "I love you, too, Matthew, but nothing has changed. You'll be back driving that truck as soon as the police get finished talking to us. Right?"

Matthew knew he wouldn't be driving it long, but he didn't want to tell her now. When he told her, he wanted it to be a good memory, not one tainted with shouting, guns, and police sirens.

She walked away from him. His heart broke with every step she took. He would have to tell her soon.

❧

The next morning Matthew pulled his pickup into Randi's driveway. The newly painted lavender door of the little house brought a smile to his face. It was another piece of evidence that she wanted to settle into a domestic life. For a moment he thought about how he had almost lost her. Not to a man with a gun, but because of his own selfishness. *Thank You, God, for showing me how much I want her in my life.*

He reached over and unbuckled the surprise he had brought for the girls.

Randi answered the door. The sadness on her face broke his heart.

"Matthew? Why are you here?" She made an attempt to neaten her hair, pushing it behind her ears. "And why is there a puppy with you?"

"I brought him for Emma. You do like puppies, don't you?" He tried to untangle himself from the leash wrapped around his legs.

"I don't have time to take care of him," Randi said, disapproval in her voice.

"I'll be taking care of him for a little while. He's just here to visit today." Matthew resisted the urge to pull her into an embrace. "Can I come in?"

Randi stepped back from the door. "Of course, but if that"—she pointed to the puppy—"makes a mess, you're cleaning it up."

"His name is Jack. He's a golden Lab, and yes, I'll clean up after him." Matthew shortened the leash in his hand to keep Jack close by and out of trouble.

"Emma's at a friend's house."

"I came to see you." He grinned at her. "I wanted to tell you something."

"What?"

"I accept."

"Accept what?" He loved the look of confusion on her face.

"Your demand."

"Demand?"

"The one you flung at me when I asked you to marry me."

"You do?"

"Yes. So can we get married now?" He reached for her hand, grasping it as he went down on one knee. "Miranda, please let me be your husband and a father to your children."

Matthew watched the emotions play across Randi's face. He could barely breathe. What was taking her so long to answer? Didn't she know he couldn't live without her? He needed her in his life every day. Then he noticed the tears welling in her eyes. "Miranda, Randi—"

Jack yelped and knocked him to the floor and began licking his face.

Randi began laughing. In a moment she said, "I think Jack wants to marry you."

"I don't want to marry Jack," Matthew sputtered and held out his hand. "Please, your answer."

"Yes."

They stared at each other for a moment. A perfect moment, Matthew thought. He could hear his heart beat in the stillness of the moment.

"But what will you do instead of driving?" she asked at last.

Matthew clasped her hand and pulled her to the floor next to him. He held her close, and she melted against him. "We'll have to move. I've been offered a ministry position at the Flannel Shirt Chapel in Thermopolis."

"Flannel Shirt Chapel?" Randi snorted. "That's the name? I guess it would make some truckers less reluctant to try it out. I haven't heard of it before."

"They're just starting it."

"You won't be driving?"

"Not at all, except to get to work."

"But your dream. . ."

"You are my new dream," Matthew said just before he kissed her. And when he did, he realized this was the dream God planned for him long ago.

epilogue

Matthew sat at the picnic table at his parents' farm. Emma sat across from him. "Emma, I'd like to discuss something with you."

"Am I in trouble?"

Matthew reached across the table and grasped her hand. "No, Emma, you're not. I have something important I want to ask you, though." He and Randi had discussed this moment earlier, but now he felt tongue-tied.

"Do I have to do something, like chores, to get an allowance when you're married?"

Emma swung her foot under the table and it connected with Matthew's leg. "I'm sorry!"

"That's okay; just try to sit still for a minute." Matthew took a deep breath. "Emma, at the wedding, I—your aunt and I—would like you to be a part of the ceremony."

"I know already. Aunt Randi told me I get to carry flowers and walk in front of her."

"Yes, but there is something else. I'd like to promise you that I'll be a good father to you, and so you'll remember that promise, I'd like to give you a ring that day, too."

"Can I change my last name to Carter like Aunt Randi?" Emma's brow wrinkled as she said, "Emma Carter. I like that name better than Emma Bell."

Matthew grinned. He hadn't expected her desire to have the same name, but it made sense. He liked the idea. "I think that would be a fine idea, Emma, but I think we should ask your dad how he feels about that."

"Maybe he'll say yes because you're going to be my newest

dad and he's my old dad. Can I get a wedding dress?"

Matthew looked into those eyes and knew she would be wrapping him around his finger by the end of the day. "A wedding dress?"

"Yes. I should have one. So when are we going shopping?"

≈

The trailer that housed the Flannel Shirt Chapel smelled of roses. Jess had worked magic to make the dark brown room special. Lilac bows graced the sides of the folding chairs, and vases of flowers adorned the small altar.

Emma twirled, and the tulle of her white dress billowed in a circle around her. "I'm getting married today!" Randi and Emma were busting with excitement when they came home from their shopping trip. Matthew even bought Emma a short veil to go with the dress. Randi smiled and then said, "I'm getting married, Emma; you're getting a dad. I think it's just about time for you to walk down the aisle, so let's get your veil on those shiny curls."

Music floated from the doorway, and Randi whispered to Emma, "It's your turn."

Emma took tiny steps, looking every bit the bride she wanted to be. Then Randi took a step inside. Her mother and Matthew's parents were in the front row. They stood, turning to watch her entrance. Randi knew Jess and Mike were there, and Brad, the driver who helped save her, but she didn't see them. The only person she saw was the man waiting for her at the end of her walk. Matthew Carter, soon to be her very own Preacher Man. Her day had come; her dream was a reality.

After the ceremony, Emma led the way out. She burst through the door shouting, "We're married!"

Randi and Matthew walked through the doorway. Matthew turned Randi toward him and leaned in for a kiss. A line of trucks led by the Groovy Grannies in their bright pink rig began blowing their horns, issuing a wedding salute, trucker style, as they circled the truck stop.

A Letter To Our Readers

Dear Reader:

In order that we might better contribute to your reading enjoyment, we would appreciate your taking a few minutes to respond to the following questions. We welcome your comments and read each form and letter we receive. When completed, please return to the following:

Fiction Editor
Heartsong Presents
PO Box 719
Uhrichsville, Ohio 44683

1. Did you enjoy reading *Hearts on the Road* by Diana Lesire Brandmeyer?
   ❏ Very much! I would like to see more books by this author!
   ❏ Moderately. I would have enjoyed it more if

   _____

   _____

   _____

2. Are you a member of **Heartsong Presents**? ❏ Yes ❏ No
   If no, where did you purchase this book? _____

   _____

3. How would you rate, on a scale from 1 (poor) to 5 (superior), the cover design? _____

4. On a scale from 1 (poor) to 10 (superior), please rate the following elements.

____ Heroine		____ Plot
____ Hero		____ Inspirational theme
____ Setting		____ Secondary characters

5. These characters were special because? _____
   _____
   _____

6. How has this book inspired your life? _____
   _____
   _____

7. What settings would you like to see covered in future
   Heartsong Presents books? _____
   _____
   _____

8. What are some inspirational themes you would like to see
   treated in future books? _____
   _____
   _____

9. Would you be interested in reading other **Heartsong
   Presents** titles?   ❏ Yes   ❏ No

10.   Please check your age range:
        ❏ Under 18   ❏ 18-24
        ❏ 25-34   ❏ 35-45
        ❏ 46-55   ❏ Over 55

Name _____
Occupation _____
Address _____
City, State, Zip_____

CALIFORNIA CAPERS

3 stories in 1

At first glance, Finny, California, looks like any other coastal tourist village, but for resident Ruth Budge, the kaleidoscope of zany Finny citizens keeps her on the lookout for trouble.

Mystery Collection, paperback, 464 pages, 5³⁄₁₆" x 8"

Heart♥ong

Presents